Born in Harare, Zimbabwe, Tawanda Chabikwa grew up in both the city and rural areas. After his initial scholarship to attend the United World College in Hong Kong, he traveled broadly absorbing cultures and creative processes. As a young contemporary artist, he also works with visual media, painting, sculpture, sound and performance. Along his journey, Tawanda has attained his BA in Human Ecology from College of the Atlantic in Maine and his MFA in Dance from Southern Methodist University in Texas. This is his first novel.

D1522111

ISBN: 1451504608
ISBN-13: 9781451504606

Baobabs in Heaven

a novel

Tawanda Chabikwa

Voices in the Desert

The first poem I ever wrote was an ode to my little brother. He passed away when I was well, young. He was younger. The circumstances surrounding his death formed themselves in my mind to create a world of magic and mystery. I was consumed by the gyre of dreamtalk. I remember he looked like he was asleep in the coffin. Blue baby regalia donned and surrounded by the white silk cushioning. It was a small coffin. There were candles at either end of the mini-casket and a dreary tablecloth. The living room had been successfully transformed into a mourning room. The carpet took on the hue of blood red sand. And the walls, painted off-white, created a vastness of the little space. A privately public desert was created and it became the wasteland engulfed in moans and sniffles and occasional out of context wails from the overweight women who were tumbling about. Actually they were seated in one spot and swaying, but their tumultuous buttocks (and everything else) made them appear to be rolling all over the room. These were the ladies whose presence I never understood at funerals. One such woman was rocking from side to side seated in the darkest corner of the room. She let out a yelp that came as no surprise to those used to funerals. After this ejaculation came a dribble of mumbles from the same woman about how the Lord should have taken her instead of an infant. How life

1

was unfair and the Lord's ways a mystery to a humble believer. The women who sat about her muttered mutedly in agreement. Those nearer to her attempted to put their arms as far around her as possible. This was the cue that raised the hymn.

A coarse-voiced woman raised the raspy lament with solemnity that was the epitome of sorrow. She was also swinging her shakers dejectedly. Both were held in the firm grip of her left hand as her right supported her seated weight that leaned to one side. Her chin was raised for the first line which she then surrendered to the willing voices of the rest of the people seated in the blood red sand. The desert became alive with the sound of song. This was not the clean sound of orchestrated music. The song was built by voices searching for each other in this private desert, which when they found each other would walk in pairs or trios. The voices continued to join up and reach out to find the other stray ones. By the end of the first verse of the hymn, they were all together. This sound carried with it the beautiful imperfection of life. I felt that all who sang did not need to be here to mourn my brother. It was almost as though a breeze was blowing through the room as they sang.

A slow line of people filed into the room, past the coffin, around and out again. It was like a large snake. They were going past to see my brother once more before he was committed to the damp darkness. I watched as the people went by. Each one changed after they saw him. Women would shudder, sigh and move on. The men kept their palms joined in front of them as they walked or made soundless clapping to the tempo of the hymn. There were those who would look at the body and be completely undone. I was curious to see what he looked like. Death does things to people.

I went first and Jeremiah followed behind. I stood over the coffin for what seemed an eternity. He looked like he was asleep...only, not breathing. The music became a lullaby for him. It made him alive, frozen in *then* swept me into *forever.* These are the places where everything happens. The air became heavy and cool and I breathed in the moment. I wanted to touch him. Then Jeremiah beside me broke down and my uncle whisked us out of the room swiftly leaving my dream calling to return. Jeremiah cried. I was unyielding, as though I had learned to trust a stone from the day I was born. I wanted to see my brother.

I remember seeing my father – years of sadness taking from him - seated outside with the other men around the fire. First his wife in childbirth, now the child she had died giving life to. Years of sadness engraved in his face. He wore a navy green coat to fend off the early morning chill. The men around him, friends from church, sat in silent solace. Men do not talk. Some things remain the way they are and are good that way. Words create a distance. My grandmother sat indoors. *Ambuya.* The women had spread their wrappers on the floor and sat on them. They had their shakers, hymn books and bibles with them. They hugged and touched. They talked in proverbs, they created dreams. They sat in their individual worlds and came together to make song. Women sing. I walked about doing nothing much...I was a child.

* * *

Rapturous stains

Usually, the sunlight streams in thinly through the window, thoughts flow out of my mind onto the paper. Rapturous stains of ink emerge. The pen is guided in its mal-practice by a mightily frail hand. With it I conduct a personal orchestra of woes, whose unending symphonies become medicine and hope.

For those who sit and wait in the cool depth of silence, living off the scraps of lies. Our fathers stand on peaks of monstrosities that become our skyline and our aspirations. Babies cry as they suckle at the dry nipples of social existence. Brickwords crumble against the fortitude of government buildings like the dry blood of forgotten freedom fighters that cakes the famished soil. The pool of people's sweat is the breeding ground of the governmental mosquitoes that feed on native pawns. Knowing that I did not stand amidst the cheers and bright lights as great hands were shaken above our heads. I was in a little red room as it were. But the dust does not lie.

A silence is shouts into my ears. Even the touch of her palms does not silence the nothingness. My breath plucks at the chords of the empathetic air. She does not like it when I "go inside".

"Where are you?"
"Inside,"
"Inside…"

"I feel myself expand so that I become the universe, and everything is within me. I feel my self extend outward to the point of implosion."

There is silence for a long time. Then, I say

"It is good that you are here when I come back." That is all she needs to hear.

Tonight on the porch of her house I sit staring at the silver sprinklings in the heavens. The night is as black as a Nubian dream. Yet the sky is filled with stars. They have a ferocious brightness. It looks like a frenzied celebration of life in the sky alone. The stars look so alive. As if they know some covert truth that gives them eternal joy. The chair is a large reed framework with cushioning so outsized, I almost sink in it. I am holding a mug of warm water in my palms, it keeps them warm. Lee is rubbing my shoulders. I look up at the night sky.

'The sky is always nearer at home', that is what I have told people. The moon invites you to share a meal with it. The clouds are so low you can touch them. All you need to do is climb a mountain and you may sit and laugh with them. When you raise your palms up to the sky the sun bows over and kisses them. And when the sky is near, there is reason to hope. There is room to dream.

It is easier to sleep when the sky is near. The dreams hover right above you. The garden chair creaks a little as I tilt my head to one side. She picks up on the hint and rubs the other side of my neck.

"Have you written lately?" she hits the mark.

"I am a writer, I am supposed to write. But I am *not* a writer. Besides people read things and it doesn't make much of a difference. With all these things going on nowadays, who cares what there is to be written? Everybody is lost in desperation and fiscal urgencies. I can't write, I don't feel like it. There is much more to today than people see, but how do you tell that to people who are trying to feed themselves..." I realize that my voice is getting louder.

"And it angers you," she says, calm as always.

"I had a dream, Lee."

She waits for me to go on. Her hands carry on their own conversation with my neck and shoulders.

"I saw a man, walking, there was music, something simple but old, traditional. And it was sadness and loneliness. Then I saw a fire. I think I was the man then. But people were sitting around the fire, old men. I knew them from before. They did not like me, but I ...I don't know. Then I - or he - was walking again. Sad and darkness. But familiar." I stop. An unkind warmth is rising within me.

A vehicle passes by somewhere not too far from here. There is the usual peace of a low-density suburban nighttime. This is where Lee lives. All alone in a big house with a vast yard. It is in the more plush of neighborhoods about twenty minutes outside the central business district. Like most suburbs, there is not even the glow of the city. The lawn off the porch is well nourished. There is the helper, who sleeps in the quarters behind the main house. The night watchman presumably spends the night awake at the gate. A guard dog roams the grounds. It is a safe neighborhood. The Neighborhood Watch strolls about nightly, pummeling any unfortunate, loitering blighters. Lee is John's 'unique' acquaintance. I would call them boyfriend and girlfriend, but I have no use for the terms in my everyday living. But basically, they have a 'thing' going.

I met Lee in a Cultural Studies class in university a few years ago. She dropped out after two classes. I saw her at lunch one day when she stood in front of me in the line. I asked her about the class and she outlined all the reasons I should not be taking that class. This led us through a conversation that showed us why we would never be compatible, and that we both completely lack what the other has. Because of this mutual incompatibility, we became friends. I guess a lot of it had to do with my malleability. We came to terms with subtracting the plausibility of formal intimacy in our friendship, besides she is too pretty. I am repelled by prettiness. So we are very close friends.

Then there was John. He came to terms rather quickly, with Lee's closeness to me. So John and I engage in masculine endeavors occasionally. I like John and Lee because they are very relaxed and do not leech onto each other like some couples do. This also means I get my fair share of Lee, at least till they decide to marry. Tonight is another night I will spend at her house. Because her home is "too big" for her and John is "not yet ready" to move in with her, I can smuggle some luxury into my life. Her father died and her mother is living in Singapore. Lee insists on staying in Zimbabwe, so she has the four bedroom mansion which I invade when my place becomes unbearable or when she asks me to hop over. I bring my tools with me and write when I can, but sometimes, like tonight, I do not feel like writing.

I pull Lee round to the front of the seat and bury my face in her soft warm stomach. I put my arms round the back of her thighs. She kisses my forehead like I am her child. I let her go slowly. There is always sadness when I release her. I do not know whether it is hers or mine. Her night pants hold onto her thighs loosely. Her silk top looks like something her mom sent her from Asia. It has an angry looking dragon curling itself fluidly on her sternum. It is a murderous red and the dragon is a mahogany black-purple. Her pants are silky, Prussian blue. The color of the night. Rubbing her calves up and down, I sigh heavily. I like her legs. Lee plays a lot of tennis, and she is quite the swimmer. Her calves are full and strong. I salivate slightly at the thought. She is still holding my head. I squeeze her calves.

"So, tomorrow is Saturday," I sigh.

"Yup, and you're going with John to the farm,"

"What farm?"

"To get meat, and don't act like you have anything better to do with you life."

"I'm glad you think so highly of me," I mumble.

Lifting her onto the seat, I snuggle back into the cushioning. I put my arms around her. She sighs as I kiss her shoulder.

"This is a pretty big chair," I say.

"Yeah, my mom has a knack for comfort," her tone is exaggerated.

She always makes fun of her mother. I smile. I allow for a few seconds to pass.

"So how are *you* doing?" I ask swaying her lightly in my arms.

"I sit across the table from my mom and watch her sometimes when I go to visit her. She relives the tedious evening rituals that she's had for forever. She can't feel that when she wakes up the next day ... that I will be gone," she stops for a moment to choose her words, "Maybe she misses me. I always leave her without saying goodbye. I think that hurting someone is an act of reluctant intimacy." She said the last part as though delivering a thesis." I like it when you're here," she sounds small and tender.

"I won't be for long when John punches my face in," I joke a little too nervously.

"You're silly..." she jabs my ribs.

We watch the stars for a while longer. The water in my mug is cool. Her breathing is soft. She places her arms over mine. Her breathing is slow and she shivers slightly.

"I like it when you're here," she says again.

* * *

The Daughter

Another story my grandmother told that has stayed with me for a long time is the story of the Daughter. As *Ambuya* sat there in the usual spot in the hut, I imagined that this daughter was a girl who bore nothing profound in her appearance. That there were girls more beautiful than her in the Village. That the only unique quality she had was the sullen clarity that I could only liken to the aloofness of a giraffe. *Ambuya* also spoke of the father of the Daughter. Her voice would swoon and dive as she relayed this liquid tale:

"She was the daughter of the Basket Weaver. Her father was a joyous man, he sat in his compound daily, surrounded by reeds of all sorts. He knew reeds well. His basketry was known throughout the plateau. People came from other villages to have him make baskets, and mats for them. He always had visitors because of his love for conversation. This meant his two wives were always busy preparing beer and food." She pauses and the tale forms behind her eyes as though from memory.

"He would sit with visitors and listen as they spoke. Strange tales had made him wiser. Through weaving he understood the intricacy of life. In the pots of water which he dipped his reeds to weave, he had watched the years accumulate on his reflection. Each year left a new crease as it passed by. He could have sat with the elders at the gatherings in the Village, but he

chose to sit on his goat-skin mat and smoke his pipe." We sat
quietly waiting for this tale to sprout tender roots in our minds.
There were six or seven of us, young and sleepy. Jeremiah was
sitting next to me.

"His daughter was young. She was his favorite. The
Daughter's story became a well known memory of the Village.
She had been sent to go and get water from the river by her
mother. The sun was going down, when she arrived. The lake
was very still and dark, it almost seemed one could walk on it.
She left the clay pots by the banks and waded into the lake.

"Then it called her out farther. She knew that sometimes
impish spirits call you out to your demise so she did not go.
She also knew that if she drowned, no one was allowed to cry for
her, because then the Water Spirit would not return her. The
Daughter's thoughts took her back to all the things her father
had told her all about the Village, this place that had been his
home. The Village in all its beauty and grandeur along with its
disfigurement and malformations. They guarded their ugliness
with insidious ferocity and only proclaimed the winsome face.

"A jolt by the water snapped her out of her senses. She was
in the middle of the lake and was unsure how she got there.
The still water of the lake had carried her there. Her heart
beat at her chest as she looked at the shore of the lake. It was
far off, longing for her return. The sun was much closer to the
horizon. She thought of her father. Drowning was not as she
had imagined it would be. The surface of the lake was as red as
the clay used to cover the skin of brides on their wedding day.
The world had never been more quiet. The lake had been waiting for her. So she was taken." We sigh at the loss of the girl.
The flames of the fire in the hut writhe a little slower and the
younger children stare in disbelief at the death that happened
so early in the tale. Grandmother continues,

"She did not disappear, she only died. Her screams and fears were numbed as she sank deeper. You cannot take your fears with you when you are taken by the water. There is no use for them in that world. It was not the *njuzu's* – the Water Spirit's will that those who drowned came to her, it was just the way things had always been since the Breath had walked over the water. So the Water Spirit welcomed her.

"The light of dusk negotiated its transition with the harbingers of night. The end of the day and that of her life had come to an agreement to meet over these waters on this day and hold hands for a while. Her lungs began to burn. Liquid orange flames burst forth from her lips. As she cried her tears were black and thick. They hung, oddly in the water. She felt her veins and ears begin to throb. Her heart swelled and pounded monstrously. Then there was pain like none she had ever known. She thought her veins were being ripped out of her arms and legs and her heart was coming up through her throat. With her eyes screwed shut she heard the sound of snapping, then felt immense warmth. The Daughter knew that she had died.

"The Water Spirit she spoke to the Daughter.

You did not disappear, she said without sound, *you only died*.

"The water undressed her. It did this so kindly it made her smile. Bangles and amulets followed. But her waist beads remained. *You are still a daughter*, said the Spirit again without sound.

"These were to be her last words for the many years the Daughter spent with her. As the Spirit turned and moved away, the Daughter noticed that she too, among the many amulets and talismans around her waist, wore the customary beads of a daughter. This gave the Daughter comfort. She liberated the rest of her anxiety and followed the Spirit into the dark water."

This was not the end of the tale, but it was time to surrender our restlessness to the night. So we shuffled out into the compound heading for our various rooms. Jeremiah and I left our footprints in the dust as we walked quietly.

* * *

Champion

The car is moving along like a limping, bow-legged child. An unreliable mirage leads the way, popping up every now and then on the tar ahead. When I am tired of watching the mirage, I roll my eyes over to the window of the passenger seat. The unyielding yellow of the elephant grass makes me feel cool inside despite the heat of the day. It is not intense heat; quite the opposite. It is more like the lazy heat of a dispassionate love affair. I roll down the window and let in a blast of friendly air. It makes me smile. I unbutton an additional two buttons of my green shirt so that my solar plexus peeps through. Moving the seat back, I remove the sandals and stick my feet resolutely on the dashboard.

"Comfortable are we? We'll be there soon, champion," this is John.

He is at the wheel of the *Toyota* Corolla, that has done its fair share of road-hogging. The car is ready to throw in its cards but John has been determined to ride it into the ground, even if it means letting us get stranded in the middle of nowhere. I had suggested we take my car, or his other car, but he had refused. So here we are bouncing about inside this tin can on a perfectly smooth tarred highway.

"Did you bring the money?" John has to raise his voice slightly to be heard over the engine.

"I brought *my* money. If you haven't brought yours, that's your own problem. You'll have to go home and tell your woman that there will be no food for a month."

"Of course I brought my money, you goat. You know that money has never been a problem for me, champion!" He speaks with such buoyancy

The farm is probably another ten minutes down the road, if my memory is correct. I am rather enjoying the feeling of being on the road despite the shaky vehicle we are in. There are cattle spread sparse across the landscape outside. They barely notice us pass and most have their heads deep in the grass. One or two look blankly at the highway clearly bored to the core as they chew. Others are lying on the ground with impossible parts of their bodies twitching at different times. We turn into the final stretch of our journey through the rickety gate posts. The termite-ravaged unfortunates are each twice the size of a man and lean treacherously inwards. We are now officially in the farm though we have been driving alongside it for half an hour on the highway. The next five minutes are almost unbearable. We may as well have been put in a barrel and kicked all the way to the kraals.

Road unending, on and on alone on the road. No sun in the sky, no sky on the earth, no shadow. A timeless journey to nowhere.

"You need to get rid of this piece of trash, *ferrah*!" I yell pulling myself down in my seat.

"Chill out, champion. The worst is over!" cries John, clearly enjoying the experience in all its hilarity. He pushes down on the gas to aggravate the bumpiness of the ride.

"Next time we should come in a tractor." it is clear this is the only creature that can make it across this stretch with minimal damage being done to the driver,

"Slow down, you bloody cock." I yell as I am thrown toward the roof of the car by a particularly overzealous lurch of the vehicle.

Finally, we roll into the opening, and see three men in green overalls and dejected Wellingtons, herding the cattle into the kraal. We are just on time. I get out of the car, stretch my arms out and yawn. Then I rub my behind to check for damage. The fresh odor of cow dung swims into my system. A strange relief greets this smell. At the scent of moist earth, I begin to salivate and I feel a tickle in my ears. The cattle are moving reluctantly, like oversize boulders in a powerful river being swept along. I can not see the force that drives them though. It certainly is not the boy of fifteen or so, who holds a leather whip on a flexible stick at least twice his height. The cattle know where to go and their motion is almost regal. There is no need for the whip.

"We've come for meat." John is never one to waste time. "How does this work, my brothers?" as though he does not know.

"You can only choose the ones with the blue tags on the ears," responds a man about as old as ourselves.

"Champion, come and see." I stride over taking my sweet time. "Blue tags only, he says." John is already on the roll. "Let us in… to choose," "Are you sure you want to go in?" The man is surprised. People usually do not go in the kraal to pick their dinner.

"We know what we are doing," John says, already climbing over the wooden fencing framework.

He lands squarely on his feet and sinks a little in the dung. The farm workers look on, half-expecting a yell of disgust. They are disappointed to see this city man continue as though he has been doing this all his life. I follow him in. The cattle are not too alarmed by our presence. We walk among them and look.

"How about that one?" suggests the worker who walks behind us.

"It is ill," I say, barely looking at the animal. This startles him. John smirks and lets out a half-cough-half-laugh.

"How do you know this?" says the man, testing me. He sounds slightly offended.

"Look behind the ears," I say, not bothering to wait for him to do so. Sometimes these blokes try to sell you a bad cow, sometimes they are honestly mistaken. He is honestly mistaken, but he handles it well.

"You've spoken the truth, sir," he admits after looking behind the ears of the cow.

"Don't challenge him," John warns the man laughingly, "he may be from the city, but he knows how to choose his meat. Aren't I right, Champion?"

I stop in front of a young bull. It is thick-skinned with savory musculature. Its nose is moist and its tongue is smooth and purple as it licks its nose. It has a clear look in its eyes and the mucus that gathers in the corners of its eyes is of continuous tone. The fur is smooth and reflective despite the dust and dirt it has accumulated from its walk to the river in the morning. The young bull looks up at me indifferently and swivels his tail. He flares his nostrils and grunts. He is lazily chewing cud. The eyes are glazed over. This juvenile bull lacks character, but it is fit.

"This one," I say resolutely.

One of the workers who has been sitting on the fence chewing a blade of grass jumps down, puts a rope around the bull's small horns and leads it out. John is pulling out his wads of bills from the little bag he has brought. They are wound in bundles by rubber bands. I pull my half out of my shorts, glad to be relieved of the weight. The men look greedily at the money and one of them comes and receives it with shaky hands. John's bulk seems enormous before this bony character. I throw the bundles of money at the man as he is approaching me. I remember him from the last time we came here. It must have been at least three months ago if not more.

He is the oldest of the crew, and clearly the most respected, by virtue of age than anything else. He is skinny and at the stage in life when you begin to shrink, the gray stubble on his chin sticks out as though in protest. His tempestuous side-burns give a hint of an equally violent mat of hair under the piteous blue hat that is generously ventilated by moth-holes. His overalls sag sullenly at his waist. Despite all the signs of fossilization setting in, the fellow has a springy youthful step. The only thing I can possibly attribute this to is a very healthy sex life. He probably has three wives and twenty children in some mundane compound in the nether regions of the vast farmland. It would be the same with all the other workers.

"There is enough for a beer each, for the three of you as well," I mention with a hint of mischief, "and bring two out for me and my brother here. One *Castle* and one *Zambezi*." I name the beer brands John and I enjoy respectively.

"Thank you," he says, with a grin that heralds the need for a dentist's attention. "You heard what the man said." he yells over his shoulder and another young man jogs off to the building where the store and butchery stand together.

"Hey, big man," John shouts after the jogging man, "when the bull is done, tell them we want the liver and the heart out here, and bring a grill with wood. You know the drill..."

This refreshes the old man's memory and he points at us alternately with the bundles of money.

"You have been here before, no? Same thing every time, there are not many like you who would spend time with us to talk or get us a beer. These city folk just come for their meat and they leave, no time to breathe even. I knew you looked familiar!"

"That is how to live together as kin," I say, "What is it worth to be settled when your brothers are thirsting?" I piece together this phrase on the spot, and it pleases the old man.

"You have spoken Truth. Allow me to go and relieve myself of this weight in my hands. Whether I put it in the cash register or the rubbish bin, it makes no difference these days, huh?" he bounces away with his heels never touching the ground.

The Toyota creaks and makes a perplexing sizzling sound. John and I turn and face the vehicle. I look at John and say nothing.

"What is it, champion?" he asks feigning innocence.

"Don't give me that shit," I yell "You're lucky no one else was here or else they would have given you back your money and told you to go fix your car."

"You need to relax, champion. Life is thus."

None are fooled by John's resolution to refer to me as 'champion'. If anything, I am quite the opposite of a champion. It is simply a term of endearment. Men have come up with a lot of these terms to compensate softness they will not admit. 'Champion' is actually more commonly used as an ironic term for a loser, defined as: One who does not don underwear. The pronunciation of the word is a bastardized rendition of the word with the first and last syllables of the word. In response, I decided to christen him "Ferrah". The history of this word is as foreign to me as Azerbaijan, but it does the job.

"You have any idea how much a farmer makes these days?" John's eyes light up at the thought of profit, "Take the Boer that owns this piece of land here for example; half the money we paid goes straight into his khaki shorts."

"Well, I hope it's *your* half that ends up there," I avoid such topics with a passion.

"Seriously, and the rest is shared among fifty of his workers."

"At least we'll have bought them some booze," I sustain my disinterest.

"Wouldn't you like to have one of these?"

"Not really."

"That's because your testicles are like those of a field mouse!" he disguises his annoyance with humor.

"Hey, those things reproduce pretty quickly."

The man returns with our beers. They are well chilled. And the label is peeling off mine. The other two come carrying a rusty grill between them. It is loaded and ready to go. John sits on the bonnet as they light up the grill. I open the beer with my teeth. It lets out a sigh of gratitude. I take a sip. John dives right into a discussion about politics and the men are grateful that someone actually cares about what they have to say. John was a law major in university but has become a businessman by profession. Politics is his topic of choice as it is with most urban Zimbabweans. It always exasperates him that I refused to talk about it, and about Lee, and about anything that is not intellectually personal.

All alone just a feeling within as the road turns to tar, as the gravel disappears, leaving only the hope of footprints. But none are left.

The men drink their beer in a restrained fashion. They are visibly pleased to move away from the cheap, traditional brew for a while. We drink and talk. Two groups of people come to buy cows as we sit there with the workers. The second group is of two women and a man. We exchange greetings with the man, and the bulkier woman. The other woman ignores us or does not hear us. John invites the man to join us while he waits, but the thin woman gives him a severe look so he declines. The worker who had gone to take care of them returns after having run around the kraal pulling moody cattle about for display. He looks rather flustered and rightfully annoyed.

"Take a sip, my brother," John mocks, "you have worked hard." We all laugh at man; he is the youngest in the group.

"It's just part of the job," he says, "and this is not even the worst. Some customers act like they want us to kill the cow so they can look at the meat before making a decision! At least you guys climb in and choose for yourself." He helps himself to a large gulp before passing on the quart.

The man who has come with the two women goes off to buy some drinks. The women sit in the car and wait while listening to the radio and chattering about everything and nothing. The man returns and gives the women their drink. He proceeds to approach us.

"I feel sorry for him," says one of the workers and we all laugh.

He comes up to us and before long has joined in the conversation. Apparently he is doing his mother a favor by driving up to buy meat for the thin woman's wedding. And the heavier woman is just an unfortunate friend. He says he is not about to be the one to break the news to the bridegroom that he will be marrying a golden-faced bitch.

"I'm always skeptical of the pretty ones," I enterprise on the opportunity to voice my opinion, "if I ever marry, it'll the butt-ugliest mess-of-a-girl you ever did see."

The men explode into a laughter that is partially alcohol inspired. It makes the bride in the car toss us another venomous look.

"I'm serious," I do not relent, "she'll be so ugly that even I won't want to spend the night with her," more laughter, "It's a win-win situation, you see: she needs someone to marry her, and I don't want to worry about other men sleeping with my wife."

From there, the conversation deteriorates into adult tomfoolery. It is mid-afternoon and many laughs later when we leave.

* * *

Remember me

Stories of love resonate in our lives, like the sound of the ocean in a large seashell. I have thought of why this is so: That as the winds blow through the shell, a once fêted reality is unfolded, lifted from the depths of forgotten selves. The selves that were whims of our growth. Jeremiah and I outgrew the monotony of the little village that was a world in its own right. In it, we exchanged the formal farewells as we were herding cattle in the savannah. The forest never ceases to whisper secrets. Our voices became a part of the stories that would travel with the wind. As we walked behind the cattle slowly, he asked me many questions for which I had no answers. I promised to write him a letter from the city with all the answers. I also promised to visit frequently.

It is true that the remote village was burdened by the unholy ignorance that smiled ever so graciously upon its people. Their faces faded in a cloud of dust behind me as the rust-bucket bus stole me away. The dust raised by the rickety vehicle closed like a ghostly fog curtain. Everything disappeared but Jeremiah. He disobeyed his small legs and chased the bus waving and shouting. But he could only follow for a while before the curtain fell over him too. We had said goodbye with firm handshakes and pats on our sun-darkened backs as parting gifts.

"Remember me." he had said, giving me these words as though he were passing me a fragile gift wrapped by his own skin.

Today, I see the unspoken gratefulness on his time-ravaged expression. I did not forget him. I have grappled with a weakening memory and have rescued his image from the swirl of eventuality; I come to resuscitate it in my mind – to make him real. As we sit in a timeless space without sound, I am trying to fight the change. I watch Jeremiah look at me, a grin slides over his rough face and the twilight shines in his iris. It is as though he is the resting place of the sun.

"What news from the city?" he asks, clearly not interested in the answer at all. He knows that I come not to bring news. I come because I have nowhere to go.

"They are all well in the city: Smiles one day then tears the next. You know how it is. Some things are bound to remain the same. I am here to receive the news from *you*."

Everyone knows that it is in the country that all the excitement lives." There could be no lie more obvious.

It is amazing how eyes remain the same. He is still the same boy I left standing in the dust road behind me as the bus coughed and spat its way to the city. The contours of his face hide nothing of the turmoil of rural life. Yet he has borne it so well. He is reinforcing his cattle whip, a flexible sapling of the *mutondo* tree, about three feet long. It has been peeled to reveal the core that is now brown with age. His Herculean forearms are tying a braided length of leather to the end of the limb with a thick rubber band. His strong arms are calloused. His nails are dark brown. Veins are enclaved in a labyrinthine design from his elbows down to his knuckles. I wince at the thought of being the livestock that will be lashed by this weapon. I rise from the brick and dust off my pants. The sun continues to glide towards its end.

"Where to, *shasha*?" Jeremiah looks up raising an eyebrow, "the women are cooking."

"Let's stretch our legs," I am sure he knows where we are going.

We speak very little. It has always been that way, but there is a place where speaking can not be avoided. We trudge down the road walking toward where the sun sets. The sand on the road is getting cool, I can tell when it is caught between my feet and the sandals. Young girls are walking with buckets and pots of water balanced on their heads. Young boys are herding the cattle back to their homes. Men are walking back home from the fields with hoes and mattocks over their shoulders. Women are walking in groups from their gardens. Jeremiah greets each one, I follow suite. We call out a greeting occasionally as we pass homesteads where the elders are outside. It is getting darker. As we pass by one home, Jeremiah sees the mother of the house outside. She is washing a squirming, displeased child in a big metal tub.

"It is evening." he calls out in greeting, "Has the day been good to you?"

"Is that Jari?" the old lady confesses her weak eyesight.

"Yes it is, mother," Jeremiah makes himself known.

"Where are you headed at this time when the livestock is going home?" she asks, truly concerned. Such are the concerns of the old ladies. Only illness or death would make them budge from their dwelling place when darkness is upon the land.

"kwa*Maraki*." Jeremiah shouts out. There is no turning back now.

Maraki is the Africanized version of the biblical name, Malachi. This is the name of the village entrepreneur: owner of the bar, the store (which really just sells cooking oil, salt and sugar) and the diesel grinding mill. True, there are a few other business-minded folk, but not within a forty-kilometer radius. And so we arrive. In agreement with the unwritten laws, I buy beer for everyone there. The stereo blasts away and we sing and watch the drunker ones dance. *Maraki* sends off two of his kids to spread the news of my arrival. I wonder whether this is in good faith or a ploy to boost his business. It is probably both. The dusty little boys return with throngs of people, all men of the village. They bring with them empty pockets and big, thirsty grins. They call me "city boy" much to my annoyance. The music pummels our ears and the night finds its way to the village. The news travels that I am back and the bar is obliged to stay open longer. The deep laughter that I have been yearning for saturates the air. The people laugh and, in accordance with what I believe about people of the land: they are joyous. It is a while before I realize that the laughter is also coming from myself.

"You are foolish to leave the city to come join us in our suffering," slurs one of the men leaning on me heavily, "You city boys can never be weaned from your mothers' breasts, huh?" everyone laughs the deep, fertile rural laughter.

"You are foolish to come to the bar to see me," I retort, "as we speak, your wives are moaning to the thrusts of some boy without pubic hairs." and even greater laughter. The man slaps my back and returns to the dance floor laughing.

The laughter runs deep and true like a raging river. It refreshes the lime memories engraved in our bones by the stories we were told as children. We laugh at each other alternately, then at the past, then at the night itself. Tired and pensive, Jeremiah and I take to the gravel road and head back home. The time does not matter. I am now in a place where the only day that matters is Sunday. Every other day folds under the weight of indifference. Jeremiah has had his drink so his tongue becomes lighter. He tells me many things about who has gone, where and when and why; about who had died, or lived; about many things. We walk down the road herding memories back home. I laugh at the emptiness of my pockets. When I arrived, they were swollen. But I bought candy for Jeremiah's children, and gave money to his wives for the children's schooling and groceries. And of course there was the bottomless well that I tried to fill at the bar.

We exchange secrets with each other and stories of our personal failures. I walk next to this man as though time has passed us by without notice. As the darkness of the early hours of the morning envelopes us, we speak in sullen, drunken voices. We become vague figures dissolved into the night. I feel as though I am walking with Night itself as it tells me the stories of many men. I listen and my mind frees itself to the vast darkness and creates shapes that rise and fall all around us as we walk. The figures disintegrate as they dive, or they linger like the ghosts of the unborn. We both fall silent.

"Do you remember the stories *Ambuya* used to tells us, Jari?" I venture into that forgotten place. "Do you remember how scared you were of the creatures she created?"

"You were the one who was afraid." We gift more deep laughter to the night.

"They were foolish stories..." I utter to myself.

"She was a good woman," he says so that not even a stranger can dispute.

A slight breeze comes as though someone has walked past me. It gives me a strange comfort. *Ambuya* always walked with a bent back and without a cane. It would have been difficult, and almost sacrilegious, to imagine her as a younger person. The only suggestion of her having been younger was the shock of hearing my mother call her *amai* (mother). To think she had been someone's mother. Her eyes were stained by age and graying out about the edges of the iris. These eyes, that could have fooled any medical practitioner, could see better than any I knew. They could see beyond the horizon and beyond today. Her facial expressions were but fractals and permutations of her many wrinkles and contours. At her sternest moments, her voice would retreat into a whisper. She was the one who taught me how to keep a secret. Each dawn, her presence was made manifest only by the graceful stealth of her aged footsteps and the therapeutic rhythm of sweeping.

"She found her peace," Jeremiah sighed.

"True...I think she had waited a long time to leave."

Her silence and her secrets now blow in the reminisces of the winds. It is a pillar of dust; that memory of mothers.

* * *

Anamorphous Shoe Cloth

I get up from my desk and look out the window of the study. It is a nice night for writing. The orange glow of the street lamp shines morosely through the curtain. There is a man staggering down the road, drunk. He leans against the street lamp, relieves himself and moves on. I like Night, it is safe and quiet. You can share secrets with the Night. It took me a while to learn its language and to learn how it befriends us. I turn from the window and face the table and stride to my seat. I sit down and begin to sigh, but I stop. There is throbbing in my ears.

As night crept into the cave, his dreams crouched in the darkness. They were waiting.

My apartment is largish: two bedrooms, a bathroom, a living area, a dining space, kitchen and a pantry. I have a television without an antenna. I only watch movies on it. If there is anything worth watching, I head over to Lee's and watch it there. It is a middle density suburb that is actually closer to the high-density side. I was lucky to land a deal with the owner of this house, because he is a patron of the arts and I am a writer.

Words have become meaningless. If I try hard enough just for a second I can imagine myself to be illiterate. I can stare at the words on the walls and see them as obscure markings. For this one second I can feel an unbelievable freedom of being. It is similar to the feeling of being naked and not caring. But just as I begin to revel in this ignorance the obscure markings on the computer screen play out their anamorphism into words that I comprehend. Once more I am caged in open skies. My fingers glide over the keyboard softly as though begging the screen to give me something of worth. They have a relationship all their own with the keyboard. Sometimes they dance upon it like lovers prancing in a meadow sharing laughs. Other times, they argue with it. Then they begin to beg. Sometimes I catch myself watching my fingers, totally oblivious to what is on the screen. And when I look up there is a story … miraculously.

That was not me… just things I have done.

My eyes shifted from left to right as the question forms slowly in my mind: *"Where am I?"* It is a familiar feeling. I have been lost before. It was not too long ago. I was strolling in the city. I often go on these walks in the hope of getting lost. I want to see things happen, that I have not seen before. The city is alive with stories. By walking and losing my Self in these stories, I want to breathe them in and be submerged in them. So I can return drenched in the truths of experience.

On that day I had walked with this hope in mind. It was in June, the winter. The Zimbabwean winter actually takes place between three and eight each morning. The rest of the day is the same as any time of the year. So the sun was overhead and it was warm and dry. Every building was wearing its winter coat of dry red-orange dust. A little wind was sprinting around the city causing nothing but annoyance by throwing pieces of litter at my knees and specks of dust at my eyes. I could tell it was lunchtime because people were roaming the streets with lunch boxes or boxes from the fast food places. Walking the distance of one block I heard the word *mari* three times. This is the term for money. That is all that is on people's minds.

I could not tell what street I was on because the street signs were missing. Apparently they are made of aluminum, which is valuable for something or the other. So occasionally someone borrows them. Unfortunately, it only takes so many borrowings before there are none left. The wanderer (such as myself) is therefore left unassisted in finding his bearings. I stood at a street corner and was stunned out of my thoughts by a young fellow who attacked my suede shoes uttering, "Shoe shine, shoe shine," as he swung his shoe cloth at my feet. But I was too quick for him. I leapt a foot into the air.

"No thanks, *shasha*." I said with a warning in my voice.

"Just fifty, brother," said the chap realizing he had lost a customer.

I walked off without responding. It is an experience that one can only foresee if they have heard the stories of the street dwellers who linger at street corners in the name of shining peoples' shoes, when all they actually do is smudge your shoe before you say anything. You are therefore left with no choice but to let them clean up the smear or equally smudge your other shoe so it will at least appear symmetrical. Either way you will have to pay. I turned and looked at the fellows as I crossed the street. And I saw three of them laughing at the one I escaped. They all had filthy cloths over their shoulders and cans of all sorts of polish (or pigments) at their feet. I smiled at my victory.

Commuter vans moved at amazing speeds with equally amazing recklessness up and down the roads. I made my way to the other side safely and recognized the park. I walked up to the rows of vendors by the entrance. These folks are, in my opinion, the apex of the irrational. Their whole life is one big extreme sport, the sport of Civil Disobedience. They are ready, at each moment, to pick up their boxes and flee the Municipal

Police. You can never tell just by looking at them, their athletic prowess. They range from dreadlocked, skinny, dope-heads to obese, maternal entities. I have, on two occasions, been privileged to be in the wrong place at the right time.

The sequence of events is always the same: The lorry swerves onto the scene with several policemen adhering to it in treacherously acrobatic positions. They fly off the vehicle in the three seconds before, during and after its instantaneous stop. They wield batons and *chamboks*: the ordinary law enforcement weapons of colonial times. They are hard, black, rubber whips that flex and relax ever so dexterously as they dance on one's skin. They indiscriminately transform African backs into not-so-ancient tablets that tell of a failed escape from the agent of law. The red-eyed enforcers charge forth, virtually drooling, as they destroy anything in their path. Yes, I have born witness to two such events. I was so surprised by sight of overweight women outrunning skinny middle-aged men that I almost forgot to make myself scarce from the scene.

Running and jumping over fences, I fall and split my skull. On my knees, I frantically gather my piteous thoughts. They are heavy. I wonder why I carry them at all.

So I bought a cigarette. He whipped out a match and lit it for me too. I also purchased a piece of gum. And walking by, a good three feet before me, was a deranged street-dweller. Had his voice not told me of his approach, his odor would have anyway. The bearded wretch reeked like a public toilet. He was dressed in a t-shirt and shorts that were once trousers. Their original color was beyond definition. They were now uniformly brown, with splurges of black. His skin was shiny black as though he had fallen into used car oil and neglected to wash it off. The hair on his head looked more depressed than I imagined Nelson Mandela to have been in his twenty-seven years of imprisonment. The few teeth left in his mouth were virtually holding up posters that implore "Get me the fuck out of here!"

A few people stopped to look at this man as he passed by muttering all sorts of things. His big beaming smile sat stupidly in contrast with the morose, reality-laden frowns of its milieu. His mutterings were impressively textured. They varied in volume, tone, and hue and were spiced up by the occasional sincere obscenity. The man was deliriously happy. The t-shirt revealed a hairy nipple and a belly button. His shorts did little to hold back a bulging scrotum. I was overcome by a strange joy.

I decided to leave my thoughts splattered all over the pavement. I continued to run. It was like being naked and not caring.

Little Stones

I listen as *Ambuya* guides us into the dark African night. Her age-old lips dance over the flames of the fire around which we sit. Time marks its own passing on rural women's naked heels and palms. The wind and the rain carve them. The women then become as mountains – immortal. Like the land on which they live, their once fertile youth becomes the arid field of the epoch that formerly defined them. But not all is lost when they become old because, as with the land, people still find comfort in it, and places to hide. People find places to rest, and they still drink from the springs and bathe in the rivers. The land, like the woman, is strong.

We have sat here many nights and have learned how to listen. The room about us slowly disappears as we readily plunge, mind-long into the world of dreams. The flames of dreamtime do not flicker, they writhe. A nervous warmth envelops us. The wings of owls begin to beat against the thatched roof, which rises above us till it becomes the sky. Our little eyes focus on Ambuya. There is the occasional sniffle from the active nose, and the scratching of an itchy face. We have taken our daily baths in water warmed by the fire. We have oiled our skin. Our shiny faces are all eyes as we stare hungrily at grandmother waiting for her to feed our minds. She waits for us to settle down.

The youngest among us do not know what is going on. They fail to comprehend the silence. Their squeaky voices continue to ask ridiculous questions: "Why are you all quiet?" or "What are you waiting for?" Some of these little pip-squeaks find it to be the opportune moment to voice their concerns:

"*Ambuya*, Tapiwa kicked me today when we were…"

"Shut up." interrupts the venomous whisper of the perpetrator amidst an uproar of pre-pubescent squeals demanding silence. We all want the story to begin.

Tonight we will swim with the water spirits. We will be abducted and apprenticed in the magical arts. *Ambuya* is wrapped, neck down in an itchy-scratchy old blanket. Yet the discomforts of the flesh are but a laugh for my grandmother. The flames sculpt her into a myth. Her arms reach out of the blanket to shape archaic gestures that guide the tale to the land in between the teller and the hearer. We stretch out the hands of our imagination and trace the contours of this tale. Passionately tragic bonds of kinship sprout in our little black hearts as thick red fertile blood traverses the canals of our longing.

The fire hisses a warning as though on cue. I always wonder how she makes that happen. The fire is in alliance with this virtuoso storyteller; it is her prop. Dreams are engraved in our minds as we breathe together. The magic of the night is drawn to our homestead. I feel it at the door. I turn and look. The Water Spirit is standing at the door. She is breathing lightly, almost not at all. She has a slight stoop in her stance, as she is not used to walking on land. Night welcomed her for they have not seen each other for a long time. Night kept her company as she walked. They talked of the many things that happened since the last time they met. Night speaks respectfully to her because the Water Spirit is older than the night.

But now she is here with us, listening. Swarms of talismans hang about her neck and waist. Through the mat of hair, her ear escapes and displays a bone piercing from which a shiny metal loop is hung. Her skin shines as though oil were rubbed over it. Bangles and cloths enrapture her wrists and ankles. She is not large and her face is the negation of age. Small stones are gathered about her feet.

I look to see if anyone else has noticed her but their eyes are all trained on *Ambuya*. The story is going on oblivious to her presence. Then she turns around and walks out just as she came. The little stones at her feet scramble after her erasing her footprints. Night follows in respectful silence. And within a few more phrases the story is over. Everyone is quietly letting go of the dream. I retract my imagination reluctantly. Some of us begin to look left and right to see each other's faces. We giggle and laugh at the few who are slower to withdraw from the trance than others. Sighs are heard all around and yawns enjoy their long awaited release.

"Why does the Water Spirit have little stones that follow her around?" my question confuses everyone there.

"To erase her footprints as she walks so none can follow her to the water," grandmother answers the question with undeniable logic.

"Mother of the House," grandfather is back. We all giggle at the familiar sound of his drunken voice. We hear him get closer; his feet are desperately trying to keep up with him.

"Can you not hear me? Mother of the House, I say!"

Ambuya waits a little while looking at us as we share in the comedy of the moment. Her eyes are as naughty as a child's. We fidget, slightly nervous, as we are all familiar with the wrath that befalls all who are slow to please *sekuru*.

"I will come!" she responds finally, much to our relief.

She slowly gets up with the difficulty of those who have spent millennia hoeing in fields with bent backs. We shuffle on the earthen floor to make room for her to pass. We hear her outside greeting grandfather by his totem – the heart. He is muttering drunkenly to himself and humming a song that no one sings anymore.

"What took you so long? And who was that woman leaving the compound at this hour?" He gestures toward the deep darkness that had consumed the Water Spirit. But the dust kept her secret.

Decalogue of Bad Toys

The night is still very much alive, and my fingers are racing over the keyboard. My publisher has been harassing me for a while now about my failure to produce "sellable" material. But I am more concerned by the itch in my ear. I sigh and turn to look over at the window. There is someone out there. At this forsaken hour of the night and in this state of mind, I barely trust my senses.

It is Lee. She is standing outside my window in a night-gown and staring at me. She is barefoot on the tarmac. There is no one else around. Lee is scratching her ear, and the orange glow of the streetlamp reflects off the silky gown, which only goes down to her thighs. I turn to look at the clock on the wall and see that it has no hands. Her ear begins bleeding and the blood drips on to her shoulder and she keeps scratching her ear and bleeding. That is when I shut my eyes.

"Fucking shit!"

It was written in the decalogue that: each creation shall leave you humble for it is never as great as your dream.

I never trust my mind. And sure enough when I open my eyes Lee is not there any more. Further down the road is a shadow. I hear a muffled scream. There on the front lawn three houses down, is the shape of a man atop a struggling robed figure. I decide to look into this. So I stride over to the desk and sip on my coffee. Then I head for the door after picking up my coat. The air is cool and there is morning dew on my lawn. As I stand under the street lamp, I realize that this is not a delusion. The man is simultaneously muffling the screams and administering sordid thrusts. I break into a jog as I near. He is slurring obscenities and heaving deep breaths.

There was an old woman who lived with her son. He used to make bad toys. He used them on people who had hurt them before.

Hearing my footsteps, the drunken bugger looks up and breathes in to speak, but my foot has the first word, which I deliver squarely in the man's mouth. He falls off the woman who does not need my permission to immerse herself -and therefore the whole street - in the murderous screams. The man is sprawled on the lawn and spitting blood and teeth out of his palm sealed lips. I feel a certain hateful relief as I conduct my vigilante justice. He covers his face so I decide to target his once virile genitalia. By now, doors are opening, as the woman continues to scream. She yells out her situation while I continue stomping the perpetrator. The crowd falls mercilessly on the man and I am pushed aside as they deliver their blows. The neighbors did not appreciate such a vile awakening. The mob ejects me amidst a bundle of excuses from the drunk. His pleads for mercy claiming to be drunk, then he claims not to have known what came over him. In a final bid, he claims to be possessed. He is silenced by kicks and punches. From experience, I know that no one has considered calling the police yet.

Some empathetic women have surrounded the victim as she sobs and moans. The Locksmith's wife has given her a blanket.

"Someone should call the police," I suggest.

"Let them set him straight first," hisses one woman who has hair curlers in place.

"But the police must know." says the Locksmith's wife; she has a rosary about her neck.

"I would urinate on his face if I was a man," says the curler woman. If it were not for the curlers she could have passed for a man.

I begin to walk back to my home.

"Thank you, brother," sobs the woman being comforted.

"It was you who heard? Son, you've done a good thing, you'll be rewarded in heaven," says the Locksmith's wife with a teary voice.

"It's a good thing you were awake, if not..."

I nod and walk away. I would bet the Locksmith is fast asleep right now. As I leave them, I hear the lady continue about urinating on his face. I realize that I locked myself out. It's good since I do not feel like writing anyway. I put my hands in my pockets and feel my car keys. The car is cold inside and there is condensation on the inside. I wipe it off with my coat sleeve. The stereo goes on with the car, and there is the voice of a female radio presenter. She says something about lonely nights, then the song begins. It is a sad love song. I flip the station to classical baroque. This will do. I think of Lee and start driving. I slow down to roll past the mob still beating up the drunk. He is now naked and bleeding, but he is moving. In some countries, they put a used car tire on rapists and set it alight. I smile at that passing thought.

Every time he used the toys, he asked, 'Mama, did you see my imagination tree grow?' His mother would say, 'They shot at a child but he did not get hurt. But the "bang" made him scared.'

I hug Lee. She is very warm and sleepy.

"What's wrong?" she mumbles.

"Nothing, go back to bed."

She sighs and looks at me. A honeyed gaze lingers in the air between us as I enjoy the remaining sensation of her fingers on my neck. She turns and goes off to her room. The air in the passage holds her scent as I follow behind her. She keeps walking as I turn into the room that I usually sleep in. The bed is made as always: a blue duvet cover and silky sheets. I go to the top drawer and pull out my pajama pants. I smile. Lee always keeps things ready for me. The sheets are cool. I will not be asleep for a while. Lee knocks on my door and walks in. She is sleepy. She walks over to the bed and slides in.

"I told you to go to bed,"

"That's what I'm doing." Her voice is as warm as her body.

She snuggles up to me, puts her arms around me and slips one leg over me.

"You're sad," she speaks with moisture that calms and refreshes even the most turbulent force.

I kiss her forehead and sigh.

"Go to sleep," I say even though she is already asleep.

The ghosts of my past visit me, and Lee's body restricts me. My desire is remitted to dense sorrow of my personal failures. I begin to have visions of the rapist naked and possessed as he claimed to be. My thoughts become a mass of ghostly whispers. Lee's face has been transformed into a secret. There are things that I will never tell and the beauty that she embodies now is one of those things.

"I'm not asleep." Her voice stuns me, "You can talk to me, you know."

"I saw a man rape someone tonight. I felt nothing when I beat him to shit." My voice is edgy and I do not like what is coming.

"What?" she opens her eyes and stares deep into me.

"Yes, I relieved the man of a few teeth. I beat him and I don't know why. They were still beating him when I left." Lee is listening now. "I saw you in my window tonight so I came to see if you were alright." I feel something break inside.

"You love me," her voice is foreign to me but her kiss is not.

I drink from her lips with a longing that surprises me. The night darkens as if to conceal our secret. Her hands explore the nape of my neck and I run down her side looking for the freedom she promises me. Her legs are wrapped tightly around me when I find my way into her silk pants. She sighs. Her eyes open wide and dig into mine. I heave a sigh and continue to drink thirstily from her lips. Her back is soft. Her moan makes my eyes well up as her soft palm finds my mast through the pants. She squeezes then suddenly lets go and embraces me. I pull my ecstatic fingers away from her center and hold her glad not to have gone any further. She wraps her legs desperately around me as I rub her back in admirable restraint. Lee is panting, silently. And her thighs are shivering. I feel the moisture on my abdomen that emanates from between her thighs. She is quiet.

"It's ok Lee," I whisper "we're good, nothing happened."

She looks me in the eyes for along while. Then turns away slowly and pulls the covers over her shoulders. She soon falls asleep. I kiss her neck gently and stroke her hair. The rest of the night I spend awake fighting my demons as I realize that her warmth is all I have ever needed. It is then that I realize that I am her weakness and she is my sanity.

How did he forget that the people he now hurt were the people he once was? There was once a boy who made bad toys.

The second wife

We arrive back at Jeremiah's homestead and sit in the kitchen. His second wife, having heard us return, comes into the kitchen, kneels and begins to make a fire for us silently. I smile at how she moves about like ghost in the dimness of the oil lamp. She is snapping a few of the twigs in the corner, poking at the dead ashes and arranging the larger logs. She tears and crumples a page of the newspaper and stuffs it under the logs. All the time she is on her knees. The waistcloth she wears is faded and she has a woolen hat on her head. Her t-shirt is at least three sizes too large and has definitely seen better days. The hut is rather small so Jeremiah sits at the other side and I sit close to the door. He is staring at the floor and lets out a cough then clears his throat a little too loudly. His wife glances up at me and meets my gaze. She quickly looks down, finds the matches and lights the fire. She blows life into it and when she is satisfied, she shuffles to sit next to the cupboards, with her legs folded under her.

"Would you like some food?" she asks in an almost inaudible monotone.

"We have eaten. Bring us some water and the meat. Then the beer that is in the pots in my house." Jeremiah is impassive.

"It will be done," and she is gone.

Jeremiah pulls out his snuff bottle from his waistcoat and puts it on the bench beside him. He rises and walks towards the oil lamp while pulling out the rolling paper. He picks up the lamp and returns to his seat. He taps a little snuff into his palm. And just as his father used to do, he pinches it with his right hand and puts it to his ready nostrils and takes it in loudly. An appropriate repetition is done for the other nostril. The remainder is dusted into his rolling paper. The snuff bottle is returned to his waistcoat. He pulls out the tobacco from his side-pocket and looks up at me.

"Are we smoking today?" He asks with a smile.

"Why not."

"This is not the same as you find in the supermarkets in the city. You may not be able to…"

"Just shut up and roll, my brother." He laughs. "So where did you find your wives?" I ask.

"The same place I found your mother, he he he!" We must exchange the joke that comes before a serious conversation.

"You speak through your sphincter, my friend."

"She is not a daughter of the village, she is a woman, what more do you need to know?"

"I'm sure she was beautiful before she met you. Did you get any of my letters?"

He says he had, including the most recent one.

"When I send these letters, I often imagine you receiving them," I say, my voice is getting slower and my tongue weightier. "I imagine you sitting under the tree outside in the compound and a dusty little fellow scurrying up to you. He wears a gray shirt at least three sizes too small."

"The little bugger was wearing a blue shirt this time, *shasha*, it looked like it had belonged to his older bother and cousins and their forefathers before them," Jeremiah laughs again,

"You remember those kids from the other side of the river? The ones who could barely afford clothes?" I nod, "Yeah, the boy was dressed like one of them."

"I imagine the fellow to be about third grade. He passes you the letter with excitement dripping out of his ears. He is fueled by his self-importance. I remember how I felt at that age when I had the privilege of being chosen to deliver a letter. The old men would send me off to the kitchen and the wife would give me some bread or sweets to thank me."

"Yes," Jeremiah sustains, "that's what I did. You writers have good imagination. I always take my time opening the letters. I dream of what is in the letter before I read it." He stands and reaches over the fire to hand me a cigarette. He sighs as he sits back down, "Age is catching up with me."

"You're just lazy," I lean into the fire and light my cigarette.

The tip catches fire so I blow at it a little. I put the other end to my lips. Sour smoke rubs my tongue gently. I am unprepared for the fracas that ensues in my lungs. I let out a ragged cough.

"You were warned," says Jeremiah puffing smoke out fluidly, "did I not say…" he does not finish as he too begins to cough.

"The laughter of the tortoise…" I taunt.

This is what people say. The story goes that the tortoise laughed at the other tortoise for having a ridiculous shell on its back yet he had one too.

"I imagine you salivate a little as you open the letter,"

"Still going on about the letters," he says.

"Time can be measured in letters, my friend."

Jeremiah becomes quiet, somber; then he catches me off guard,

"On that day the sun smiled on the land and shared the sky with a few clouds. The wind sent a breeze to tickle the bark of the few trees and a lone falcon hovered overhead. It seemed the whole village gathered there, right then to hear the news this letter had brought to me." His voice carries the stoic conviction of a shaman.

"The letters are good..." he whispers, sentimentality peeps through his voice.

"Yet you never reply," my voice is not accusing, merely stating the truth.

"Life is a long time." We stop while it is still safe.

Everything is alive in his eyes. Everything breathes, feels, speaks and loves. He does not know much of the world outside the village, but I feel he will do just fine. His wife comes back in and breaks the spell. Jeremiah and I shuffle to regain composure. She has two metal bowls and a large pot piled in one arm. The other arm carries the answer to my prayer: a home-brewed traditional concoction. The calabash is floating inside the pot. Her waist cloth seems to be tied differently. It no longer falls to her ankles but reveals her smooth brown calves when she kneels. I get a better look at her in the light of the fire which is now very much alive. She is young. Her nose is rather small, but her lips are full and healthy. Her eyes still have the sparkle of youth. Her shoulders are small and rounded and her back is strong.

"Who made the brew?" I direct the question to her.

"*Maiguru*," she responds. Her voice is humble.

Maiguru is the title of the senior wife. My mouth is watering as she dips the calabash into the beer and passes it to me. Some of the beer drips onto the earthen floor. My heart beat paces up and I feel a tickle in my ears. I reach out to receive the calabash. Already I am smiling. Jeremiah is watching me with curved lips, he snorts in amusement.

"So this is where your heart lies," he stretches the words out and nods his head.

My fingers touch those of the young woman. With unexpected cultural defiance, she looks me in the eye for a moment and with slow deliberation releases the calabash. My mind is completely on the object in my hand. The smooth wet exterior of the gourd makes me feel warm inside. I take a deep breath to seize the fragrance from this drink of the ancestors. There is a magic to any drink that has been left to ferment. Drinking it is like imbibing all the events that occurred during the period of fermentation. It is like a momentary alliance with the now and the never.

"*Shasha*, are you going to drink any time soon?" Jeremiah interferes with my worship.

I look up at him then at his wife. She is looking at the ground with a smile tiptoeing across her lips. I put the gourd to my lips and drink. As I drink the texture of the liquid is everything I have hoped for and longed for. I drink almost desperately, as though I am drinking from the lips of a lover. The beer bites gently at my tongue, its richness makes me feel slightly light-headed. Before long my face is turned up to the thatched roof of the hut, with the gourd surrendering its last few drops to my longing. Disappointed, I wipe my lips and chin, my eyes are still longing. Jeremiah groans in approval and his wife giggles. I look at her.

"Your turn, Jari," I hand him the gourd.

"It is now tomorrow," whispers his wife as she leaves as modestly as she came.

Jeremiah grunts, as he fills up the gourd from the pot. I mumble an acknowledgement.

"You look pleased," Jeremiah says.

"The brew is good," I am uncertain as to whether he was speaking of the beer.

We sit in silence for a long time, as the night composes its music. The fire continues. We pass the gourd back and forth.

I have retired deep within myself. I am in the land of waking dreams. Jeremiah is looking into the fire and seeing things that I will never know. The gourd finally scrapes the bottom of the pot.

"Your room has been prepared," Jeremiah signals the end of the day.

"Thank you,"

He walks me out of the kitchen to my room, which is at the far end of the compound next to the granary. He points out the rooms as we pass and makes known their sleeping occupants. The young children sleep with their respective mothers. And the older ones are split into boys and girls. Jeremiah has his own hut close to the entrance of the compound. The head of the household is always nearest to the entrance. The rooms are in a semicircle. My room is separated from the rest by the granary. The compound is silent. The night is deep. Jeremiah stands in front of me before the door. He looks at me for a long time then pats my shoulder.

"Forget me," his words are carefully wrapped.

He turns and walks. I watch his silhouette consumed as he meanders to his hut like a tributary headed toward a great fall. I lie awake. My blankets are coarse. They smell like earth, urine, dust and goats. The floor is hard and every movement I make makes a scratching sound. I am in one of the three brick buildings in the compound. The rest are earthen, thatched buildings like the kitchen. The two wives' buildings are the other brick buildings. I breathe the textured air as the brew is courses through my system and keeps me warm.

In moments I find my body lifting itself from the floor. As though possessed, I glide out of my room and across the compound. The sprite releases me after I have tapped ever so lightly on the door of the second wife. The door shakes a little.

Then from the other side of the pitiful barrier, a shuffling approaches. The cool morning air begins to move as the faintest hint of light can be seen on the horizon's edge. I look at the sky clearing itself up. The door swishes open delicately. This is rather amazing given the state of the door. I see her eyes emerge from the dark interior of her house. She does not look surprised.

"The children are asleep," there is a leashed nervousness in her tone.

I reach out and take her hand and guide her back the way I came. As we enter my room I reach to strike a match when she holds my elbow in the darkness and sighs her rebuke. Her palms are as I had imagined them. They are cool, small, and strong on my back. It will only be a few more years before they take on the leather-like attribute of rural wives. She, however, is young. I feel this as I pull her firmness toward me and lay her down. Her breath is warm and sour on my face. Her wrapper is easy to untie, and it is all she is wearing. It becomes the lake above which her nubile, ebony form creates a shivering island. As I explore her silky, smooth topography with the insides of my hand, I almost forget she is there. But she shudders when I find her centre. She breathes out with a quaking moan. I feel myself melt in an extraordinary flame of certitude as I release years of hunger inside her.

The light is breaking forth, and she leaves hurriedly. Apart from the light sweat on her back and forehead, she leaves as she came. I feel as though something has uncoiled within me. I am much lighter. It is almost as though I have unburdened my self in a confessional. She is the secret place where I have buried some of my misery. As I float in my room, the sound of sweeping finds its way through. She is sweeping away our footprints from the compound. The dust does not lie.

Beautiful Black Shepherds

Today is a walking day. A day to get lost in the gutters of this city. I want to breathe the diesel fumes as I walk by the road and taste the dust in the air. I want to bury myself in thoughts that do not make me hate myself nor my country for not being what it could be. Yesterday came too soon. Today is the memory of yesterday projected into the future of crumbling hopes. The memory of last night's events is swarming about me as I park my car in the lot at the shopping center. I look at the impotent fuel gauge. It is unable to hold its erection, my only comfort is that it is one of many. This fact has been consolidated by the rusting fuel queues that snake about the city blocks. Vehicles are parked nose to arse like starving elephants crossing a river. As I drove by them I realized the true irony of it all. We, the people, are seated in these lines waiting. Guarding a hope. The bread will never come, the salt will never come and the fuel will never come. Life will be measured in waiting.

Knotted tongues and fists rise in the air of souls sweating out their last moments in captivity.

The sun is unfriendly as I step out of the car. I pass a bill to a chap who is finessing me in order to "take care" of my car. He smiles as the note slaps his palm and makes a bid for more.

"Just one? Times are hard, my brother." He smells like fresh marijuana and glue.

"You haven't cared for the car yet." I walk away.

There is a row of stores; the liquor store at the end looks appealing. Seconds later I emerge from it with a pocket-sized, flat bottle of *Chateau* Brandy. It is the renowned cheapest way to get drunk. Standing in the car park, I twist the cap off and take a large swig. The burning rushes down my throat and vanishes. Then heat rises in my chest smoothly. I take another gulp, which propels a little stream of warmth up my neck and into my head. Already, I begin to see things differently.

"Breakfast is served," I sigh to myself.

A few watchful street-vendors are seated at the edge of the parking lot with their edible goods atop the cardboard boxes. The *Chateau* is placed in my back pocket as I walk to them. I can never resist the urge to buy something from vendors when the opportunity presents itself, given that they are an endangered species. I feel I am supporting a cause. One of the blokes is selling mobile phone minutes. Of course this is illegal, but then so is marijuana and freedom of speech. He walks up to me wearing dark fancy shades which are thoroughly off-beat with his old T-shirt under a retired suit jacket and his shorts that also look like they should be on pension. His hair is twisted into cornrows and pushed back as the new fashion dictates. The phone cards are in his left hand in a fan, like a deck of cards.

"Name the card, *shasha*, I got it," he whispers. The cards are half hidden in his suite jacket.

"I have no phone, man." All I want is a cigarette.

His next line was unexpected but not surprising.

"Well, brother, if you want a phone…just say so." He adjusts his shades unnecessarily and advances as though he is discussing something highly confidential. I choose to entertain him.

"How much?"

"Just two-fifty, big man." He flashes me a fancy phone and quickly returns it to the cave of his jacket.

"Not today, champion," I say and keep walking towards the other vendor.

"You know we can negotiate, brother," he shouts behind me.

After buying a cigarette I, realize I have no desire to smoke, so I take two more swigs of the brandy. I start walking and I as I do so, *I go inside.* I forget that the brandy bottle is in my hand, as I walk and sip at it occasionally. The morning sun is harsh, I undo a few buttons. I walk looking down at my feet. The walk becomes me. There is a queue of cars lined up beside me all along. Occasionally a driver shouts out at me asking if there is any fuel yet. I do not know where the line is headed, but I say there is none because it is the truth. You do not need to know for sure. Nothing will come but we will sit and wait for our teeth to fall out and our hair to grey. The Black Market becomes the new reinforcement of the phrase "black is beautiful" because it is the true provider. Government has failed. We live in a black market economy. This is why my car is running, and that is why any car on the road is running.

Rage takes root within me and I don't know where it is from. I keep walking. The nearness of the sky begins to crush me rather than comfort me. The brandy hits my lips again, and this time I chug. My pace quickens. I am thinking of the lives of the mothers that put so much effort into all they do. All the love gone to waste. It decomposes and ferments into a rich hatred, in the hearts of their children. The anger becomes an outsized firearm in my hand and I wave it around at anything that moves. Maybe that is why I felt good beating the drunk man last night. Maybe that is why I have the stain of blood on my brown trousers and a smear on my right shoe. This anger is bred. Maybe that is why the whole neighborhood came down like a plague on the man. We are a psychotic people with a history of nurtured violence. Our blood longs for more blood. Yesterday came too soon.

Unleashing their last hopes, in spasms of sordid coition amongst themselves. Piteous orgasms that reek of death in the damp dark.

Yesterday. I almost made love to Lee. But I did not. This morning I woke up and she was gone, probably to classes in the university. So I left and came to the shopping centre, I felt like walking. My eyes begin to water and begin to cry. I do not think I am that sad. I snap out of my thoughts. My sight is foggy. My eyes burn, and my nose is running. Looking around it becomes clear that there is nothing wrong with me. There is smoke all about me. My hearing comes alive and there are shouts coming from beyond the cloud.

Turning to my left I recognize the university gate as the place from which the chaos is emanating. The tear gas is becoming thicker, and figures are charging out of the gates in my direction. They are young men and women chanting and yelling as they run. Most have wet towels over their mouths and noses and bottles of water - the university survival kit. A few are running backwards and hurling stones at the cloud of smoke. My confusion paralyses me for a second, but the dog bark from the cloud jars me awake. The dogs, the fucking dogs. My legs begin to do the smart thing. A few university students, for that's what I assume they are, have already gotten past me and are headed for the city in the direction I came from. Looking over my shoulder I see a masked figure with a huge glass shield emerge from the cloud. This is the ideal time to use my brandy bottle which I am still gripping. After an emergency swig to empty the bottle I turn and fling it with all my might. It lands with a dull thud on the officer's shield.

Almost immediately a horde of these government zombie henchmen emerge from the cloud to form a black wall that rushes towards us. I realize that my innocence was erased after the release of the bottle. The sound of yells and chants blends with the crunching of boots, sandals and shoes on the gravel. The cars on the road come to a halt, and some try to make a U-turn as a swarm of fleeing people is advancing upon them. I find my way onto the tar as well and realize that I am near the back of the crowd. Running behind some woman, I turn again to measure the plausibility of my escape, only to see the canines advancing. Muscular German Shepard dogs are dragging some of the masked Riot Police along. The hounds are drooling and growling leaving a few of the students frozen with fear in a puddle of urine that will soon be mixed with blood. The officers remove their masks and wave their batons with the promise of a thorough thrashing. It is hard to tell who is drooling more, the dogs or the police. Their drug-besotted minds are clearly set on one thing.

One of the officers is particularly farther ahead than the others. The girl in front of me trips and falls flat on her face with a wail; her fancy underwear exposes her fleshy buttocks as her dress rushes over her head. I take an agile leap over her and run a little farther. On turning back I see the girl being beaten over the back by the lead police officer. In a fit of stupidity I turn back. Luckily this inspires two boys who were a little ahead of me. In a few seconds we have relieved the officer of his shield and baton and are dragging the girl along with us as the police reach their fallen mate. I have a large lump on my skull and a purple shoulder that will tell of the few moments before the other two boys got to the girl and me. The students have reached the lot where my car is parked and another girl comes and takes her beaten friend from us as we run past the wall created by the students in front of the car park.

I kill my own people ...who am I?

There will be another stand-off with the police. As would be expected, the students have miraculously produced sticks and bricks from thin air and are chanting slogans about the mothers of the riot police officers. I think to myself that this may not be the best place to be but before I can get to my car, a canister of tear gas rolls past me. My legs are begging for mercy, but I think it's better they beg from me than from the police interrogators. The students run into the stores and supermarkets with the dogs in tight pursuit. The patrons of the stores run out in confusion, only to run back in when they see the canine onslaught advance. The police employ their indiscriminate use of teargas inside the store too. This is no longer a student demonstration. It is a looting extravaganza in which I would be foolish not to take part. Bricks are being thrown at shop windows and at law enforcers. I see people heading to their favorite section of the store to do a little shopping on their way out the back door. One chap is carrying a whole leg of a cow from the butchery. Through the smoky, stinging air, I recognize the fellow as the guy who offered to care for my vehicle. Our contract is certainly not being observed.

I tried to follow, in an obedient silence, the dream that would not end in a deep dark pool.

I am finding my way to what I believe to be the back of the store, when I pass by the refrigerator section. Without thinking, I reach out and grab a can of *Castle* beer. And flick it open. I drink it as my eyes are watering and my nose is running. I stop for a while. And realize my foot is on something soft. It is the coat of a store worker. It is blue with the store logo on the left pocket. I put it on, pour the beer on the sleeve and cover my face to ease the teargas pain. I decide to run back to the entrance now that I am sufficiently disguised. The tear gas becomes thinner, and I can now breathe though I am feeling faint. I see a wall of riot police just outside the door and a few dogs barking at me. I assume my role immediately.

"I work in the store, sirs." some are already advancing with raised batons, "I work in the store, please!" My palms are raised and I fall to my knees grimacing and moaning.

I am cut off in mid-speech by a baton blow to the side of my face. I collapse to the ground in a spinning world of fuzzy stars. One of the dogs is already grappling with the store coat. I feel like I am going to wet myself and throw up at the same time. I taste the blood in my mouth.

"Leave him." I hear a voice say then cough, "He's a store worker. There's another one!" I am released and the reluctant dog is pulled off me taking a piece of the coat with it.

I am pushed behind the wall of police where I see a throng of vomiting women who had come to do some shopping only to receive a surprise riot. The tear gas had worked wonders on some of them, giving them a complete makeover, from beautiful to bestial. I wipe my face with the coat as I remove it and spit. I feel nauseous but I smile inwardly at my success. I quickly remember my role and put the coat back on and stagger to my car, which has sustained only a minor dent probably from a brick. Fumbling in my pockets I pull out the car keys. It is blazing hot inside the car and the coat begins to itch. My swollen face is throbbing and my shoulder feels like it will fall off. I need to rest. It feels like my head has been split open. My thoughts are heavy too. I wonder why I carry them at all. I begin to cry again, but this time the tears are real.

The Reed Flute Traveler

We gathered at the fireplace a few days later recalling where she had left us in the tale. *Ambuya* had a habit of telling stories in bits and pieces and from various points of view. Somehow though, in this labyrinth of dreams, we never got lost. Our minds grew into molds that would be filled with the lurid whispers. We would cast them into narratives of our choosing. The world began and ended in each tale but unlike other grandmothers, mine would tell a continuous tale in which there were many tales hidden. This night she continued, or rather, she began. The little rascals, who are always complaining and squealing, finally got the attention they yearned for.

"Who knows the story of the Night?" Ambuya asks with her grey eyes glowing orange in the fire.

"Night is very dark!" the youngest one says with confidence.

"Yes it is. But did you know..." and the story begins:

"Through sleep, Night had learned to share secrets with the dwellers of the land. It was through the dreams of people that Night had gotten to know Day. Night and Day walked on opposite sides of the river holding hands. The Reed Flute Traveler was a child of the night though. Or at least that is what people called Him for none knew where He was from. He lived in the shadows of solitary flames. This is what the elders said. But none had actually seen Him. Not even some of those who told, so well, the story of who He was. Some said the Reed Flute Traveler had fallen out with the ancestors and spirits; It was just the way things had been, that He had created his own infinite universe with umber sands and silver skies. It was a universe so vast that He had no place in it. So He traveled. He would be seen once every few generations. Or maybe you would pass right by him on a forest path and you would not know it."

I sit there and listen to *Ambuya* and breathe the delicious scent of the burning wood. This smell is sour and stings the inside of your nostrils and warms your throat. The sound of the night is an operetta of the occasional hyena laugh and cricket chirping. Grandmother tells of the goodness of the harvest in the land and how the Village was drenched in the scent of life.

"The plague came with field mice, locusts and tsetse flies. The flies killed the cattle with yellow fever. The locusts came in a dark cloud from the same direction as the morning star and beat most people to the harvest. The field mice charged in amazing numbers and broke into granaries. The Village tried roasting the locusts and eating the field mice, but their taste was putrid. The elders of the village treaded barefoot to that cave of the Oracle. They prostrated themselves before the cave on the burning red earth. Crawling on their bellies, they entered the womb of the cave and sat in the ominous glow of ashes. The Oracle was brief with them, 'As you have turned your backs to us, so have we to you.' The ancestors had spoken."

I am slipping away into the deep warmth of the tale.

"The Basket Weaver heard the drum too.". I recall the Weaver from a tale she told before.

"... was seated in the contemplative silence he had known so well since his daughter drowned," yes it is him.

I surrender to my drowsiness which brings me to another place:

The elders speak in quiet voices among themselves. They scratch their heads and shake their canes. They smear their senile oratory in the faces of the Village. At the peak of their desperation, a man that none has seen arrive stands in the grand, thick night, in the light of the fire.

The elders raise their eyes to see who it is that dares to stand before them unannounced. The Village stops their speaking and whispering as they eye the stranger whose form is fused with the night and tinted by the flame. A reed flute hangs by his side and he bears no marks or symbols of title or rank from any clan. I study the man's appearance. I look at the flute and notice that it is made of a reed I am not familiar with, one I have never seen before. I suck on my pipe, wondering if this could be Him.

The Village is silent for what seems an eternity before one of the elders, well known for his acute bitterness, speaks up.

"How might we help you, stranger?"

The elders are unimpressed by this intrusion in this time of urgency, but more so by the stranger's irreverence for the royal court.

"Shall you speak or waste our time, young man?"

"Just passing through," he responds in a near inaudible yet clear phrase, "I seek food and a place to rest."

"We have no time for beggars," the elder spits out, much to the amusement of the village.

"If you can rid us of the plague, you'll get your food and rest, otherwise be gone stranger, you insult us by consuming vital legroom," the bitter elder waves his hand at the stranger with annoyance that is slightly excessive.

Baobabs in Heaven

With a phantom smile, the stranger lifts His reed flute to His lips as he turns and walks away from the fire, the glade and into the night. The dark is transformed into sound so undemanding. The land sheds effortless tears in the sound of this melody. It flows so powerfully that it becomes a river that only the ancestors can drink from. The Village becomes a dream.

Apartheid in a Nutshell

There is a loud tap on the car window. Lifting my face from the steering wheel I see two of the riot police standing outside. The door creaks loudly when I open it. It has never done that before.

"Let's go," says the larger of the officers.

Their batons are hanging on their sides and that is precisely where I would like them to stay so I obey without question. As I step out of the car, the smaller officer grabs my collar with uncalled-for aggression and gives me a shake. His eyes are red with black veins in them.

"You know, I can beat you senseless right now and come away clean as a whistle?" his voice is as sudden and perplexing as a premature ejaculation. Besides, I'm not sure that is the best use of the whistle simile.

"I'm not a stu..." my sentence ends with the reception of a punch to the ribs and a kick to the thighs.

I am flung into the back of a *Santana*, the vehicle of choice for the police. A girl is crying while three guys are silently sitting. The short uncomfortable drive lands us up at the police central headquarters. The cell is a tight fit for the twenty odd demonstrators that are already in it. We join them. The odors of sweat, blood and halitosis become the breath of life. Most of us are bruised and battered to varying degrees. I am particularly concerned about a fellow lying in the back corner of the cell in blood-soaked clothes. We are sympathetic allow the bleeding unfortunate to make use of that precious space. The people are quiet except for a few whispers and sobs. I turn to the bars and hold on to them as I have seen done in movies. They are viciously cold. I let them go. Behind me I overhear the three guys who came in the truck with me whispering.

"In case I disappear, my name is Saxon..." he sputters through a swollen lip.

"Don't worry, my brother," the other interrupts, "they'll keep us for a few days and let us go."

"But they'll beat us to pulp first," the third is sarcastic.

Then everyone recoils from the front of the cell but me. The officer that is "clean as a whistle" is approaching the cell and doing little to conceal his incomprehensible anger. His stiff, edgy walk heralds his great potential to do a lot of damage to a human body.

"You," he says, already enjoying the imminent future, "let's go." His eyes point at me.

For some reason I feel little fear and I think this ekes the officer's anger. When the lanky officer with the keys to the cell completes his fumbling, I am aided out of the holding by a strong grip to my neck. As I stagger past the officer, a strong kick paralyzes my buttocks and I grunt. The room down the hall has a rusty door. Inside, a naked light bulb hangs over a metal table where a man in a brown suit is seated. He wears huge, plastic umber-rimmed, reading spectacles. His tie is off-center. And this bothers me. He looks tired. The room is cold, but has the smell of things that you would only smell if you cut someone open. The whistle officer shoves me before this character and stands behind my right shoulder.

"I.D." He is brief.

I dig into my back pocket glad that I had carried my wallet with me.

"What were you doing there?" He is scratching his ear in a strangely familiar way.

Almost before he the man has finished asking the question I am stunned by a blow to the back of my head.

"Answer the man!" yells the officer, before he breathes a sigh of satisfaction.

"Walking," I say, enjoying the comedy of it all.

It does not seem real, like some dark comedy with shifty characters. A trigger happy lieutenant and some secret agent guy whose tie is as askew as his mind. Of course the humor is instantly amputated from my being.

"You think this is a joke?" the lieutenant shrieks as he clouts my right ear.

I keep my cool, and this clearly annoys the man. I begin to question my wisdom. Perhaps I should play along and do the begging game again. But my shoulder hurts too much.

"I'm a writer, not a student, I was just shopping at the store." I want to be brief.

"What do you write?"

"Fiction mostly."

"Fiction?"

"Yes"

Silence. He look down at his papers, then at me.

"So why are you here?" he is impatient.

"He took me out of my car." I nod at the officer.

"Apologies," mutters the goggled character, far from apologetic.

My identification is tossed at my feet. I am speedily removed from the room, a little more respectfully this time and escorted out of the building by the frothing officer. I pity the one who will receive the beating that he was hoping to give me. I am deposited with a good-humored officer who is on his way to pick up more students from the site. He sees my swollen face.

"Wrongfully accused?" he asks.

"What can I say?" I shrug.

"Life's a bitch, no?" he emphasizes the *bitch*.

"Worse things could happen." I'm intrigued by his relaxed nature.

"Those fucking kids at the varsity...blowing shit up." He keeps his eyes on the road, "But who can blame them?"

"Keep smiling," I suddenly remember the quote, "tomorrow will be worse."

At this the officer lets out a loud laugh, like he has been waiting for it all day. He pulls off his official cap and passes it to me. I am confused. But it all becomes clear when I see a pocket-sized bottle of *Chateau* brandy taped to the inside of it.

"Take a sip, *shasha*, for your trouble." He winks while holding the cap before me, "I know that no one apologized to you."

I take the cap and remove the bottle from the tape and drink deeply. A little of my pain goes away. I study the badge on the cap as I hand the officer the bottle. The words *Pro Lege - Pro Patria - Pro Populo*, are arched above the a well fed lion. The truck lurches a little as we hit a mild pothole. He hands me the bottle and I screw the top on and tape it back in the cap. I pass the brown cap back to him and smile. The officer places the cap back on his head and taps it with a regal gesture.

"That's why I wear this cap, it serves me well just as it served you, heh?" he laughs again. This time I join him.

We pull into the parking lot of the shopping center. And I point at my car. The driver pulls up to it. There is the thin memory of the odor of tear gas. And there is a group of municipal police and riot police guarding a group of about fifty students. The broken windows of the stores are pitiable. And I see a few officers, drinking beer and eating goods from the store. I assume they are reaping the fruits of their labor. Besides they probably have the munchies after all the stuff they puffed to get psyched for this event. Two dogs are sitting obediently hoping for a bit more action. I step out of the Santana and turn to the driver.

"Next one's on me," I say.

"Tomorrow will be worse!" He is still laughing when he drives on to the group of students.

I get back into my car and think that it is probably a good idea to go to the hospital for a while. I will deal with the dent tomorrow. I wonder if Lee was at the university. The late afternoon sun is laughing at the joke life played on me today. I need to use the bathroom. The hospital is not too far away. I can wait. The private hospital would be the place to go. Paperwork always puts me off though. I have a vision of some hideous oversize nurse passing me a pile of forms to fill out. Back to Lee's would be the best option, so I start the engine and begin to pull out of the parking lot but I shove the brake pedal down to avoid hitting a man in a grey suit. I realize that there are two of them. The other is a little farther behind the first who is putting up his palm to halt the vehicle. I roll down the window realizing that these are not any ordinary men. Probably government agents, the type that you do not make jokes with. They do not need to show me any identification. The first walks over to the car very casually, but I sense the threat that precedes his approach. I can almost see the leaves of plants wilt as he walks past them toward me. My heart gives a feeble little kick. I am too tired to be overly frightened. The suit is shiny grey with almost invisible black pinstripes. He wears black shoes that are dusty but it is obvious that a bright shine lies just below. His white shirt is completely buttoned and, *goddamnit*, his tie is askew.

"Can I help you?" I crackle through my swollen lip, "I was just released from the…"

"You are the writer, no?" he voice is purposive. He has placed his hand on the roof of my car.

"Yes." And to myself I say *oh shit*.

"There seems to be a lot of discontent with the way things are in this country in your work, huh?" I can tell that this is not a question, nor is it an accusation. I wait for him to get to the point. "You are not a political commentator, nor are you qualified to speak on such matters. You understand?" He is tapping lightly on the top of my car.

I understand. I understand perfectly. I understand I should tell him that I do. And that if I don't I may end up in some cell telling someone my name in case I disappear. I nod. The man is not looking at me. His gaze is scouring the environment, the broken store windows, the group of students under guard, the fuel queue. It is impossible to tell if *he* is discontented with the way things are right now, as we share this moment in captivity, though my side may be darker than his. Perhaps he sees my head nod, perhaps he doesn't.

"That is how to live together as kin. It is good," this he says with a final tap on the roof of my car as he walks away.

His face becomes a fog in my memory as soon as he turns his back to me. He walks past his mate in the shades who immediately falls behind him. And they walk away. A few seconds later I snap out of the moment and realize that I have just been warned by the government. Well, it could just be a faction of the government…but still, I have been warned! I'm not sure whether to go to the bar and celebrate the fact that my work has been noticed, or to go home and get my passport and flee to the embassy of a random country to seek refuge. Anyhow, I am smiling through my wounded face and I think to myself: *keep smiling tomorrow will be worse.* I burst out into laughter as I get to the main road and decide to turn left and head home.

I pass by my neighbor's home to get his help with my door. He is a locksmith who works in an Indian-owned store downtown or at least he did till they got rid of him. I never cared to know the details of his retrenchment. His palms are rock solid and his nails are brown and thick from years of filing away at metal. Knocking on his door after parking my car beside my house, I hear the sound of a soccer game on the television, and the noise of children playing. It is obnoxiously loud inside. So I bang harder only to be rebuked by my painful shoulder. The man comes to the door and opens it. His look of annoyance turns to a look of shock which slides smoothly into a look of recognition.

"Champion?" John's influence on how people regard me is clear, "What happened?" he is swaying and the brown beer bottle is hanging by the neck between two fingers.

"I locked myself out, when that rapist stuff happened last night." I suddenly remember that my face is disfigured and that that is what he is asking about, "Oh, my face. Varsity strike and I was caught in the cross fire." I smile.

"Let me get my things, *shasha*, no problem." He returns with a jean bag slung over his shoulder. It is making clanging sounds.

We make our way down the road to my house on foot. It is just a few meters and the breeze feels good on my beaten body. The sun is finding its way to the horizon, and the butter storks and pigeons are flying off to roost in complex formations, like the jets on National Heroes Day that whiz over our homes on their way to the sports stadium where the bribed masses and bored factions go to watch the police show and the president reminds us why we should keep our mouths shut and follow him over the cliff. The locksmith is talking about school fees and the riot and squeezing in the fact that his children cannot go to school because of it. I pick up on the hint and begin to estimate how much I am going to have to pay him for this favor. Luckily he is a friend and many men from the neighborhood, including myself, have spent many weekends watching big football games, at his house and drinking. He has a satellite dish so we get to watch the international football games and discus politics and women. I know he will not over-charge me. We get to my house and he spills the many filthy contents of his bag onto my doorstep.

"You are sure the keys are inside?" he asks.

"Yeah, just get it open." I say.

"Ok," and as soon as he says this, my door opens and Lee is standing inside.

"What happened to you?" she is horrified, "Oh my god."

The locksmith is disappointed, to have been put out of a job. He begins to gather up his tools, but I stop him.

"You know, I've been wanting to put an extra lock on this door anyway, *shasha*." I say. His face lights up.

"No problem," he says as he rejuvenates the mess on my doorstep.

I step over it to get in.

"Hey, Lee, I forgot you have a key. Don't worry it's nothing." Her hands are shivering but she is calming down.

"Let me get stuff to clean it up," she does not wait for my response.

"You want a beer while you work, *shasha?*" I call out to the locksmith on my way to the kitchen.

"Why not, Champion!" he responds over the cling-clang of the tools.

The *Castle* is cold and I bring one out for him, he receives it and opens it in the latch on the door. I open mine with my teeth and hurt my lip in the process. The locksmith looks up and give me a toothy grin then places his beer on the floor. He proceeds to use a manual drill to bore into my door above the original lock. He is already sweating from the short stroll to the house. His beard is in patches and he is wearing a faded t-shirt with the words "World Cup Champions: France" written on it. His paunch is sticking out arrogantly from the t-shirt and he pulls up at his khaki shorts every few seconds. He is of average height and build but his stomach is the only aspect in disproportion.

"They got you pretty good didn't they?" he asks without looking up from the boring.

"If only you knew, *shasha*." I shake my head.

"Come and sit down," Lee is in her motherly mode. I obey and walk over to the living room.

"Did they have the dogs and tear gas this time?" asks the locksmith as I am walking away.

"The whole kit and caboodle," I sigh.

The Locksmith makes a high-pitched moan in sympathy followed by a sigh and,

"Those dogs…those fucking dogs."

Lee has spread a pile of things on the table that I had no idea were even in my house: wads of cotton wool, antiseptic, band aids, painkillers, and little scissors.

"Where did all this come from?"

"Here and there," she says.

"You've been stocking up my house again, haven't you?" I accuse her.

"Well, someone's got to do it, and it's a good thing too. I just thought I'd repay the visit." She gets to work as I am sitting on the couch beside her.

I wince and moan, while I secretly enjoy the attention. We are quiet as she dabs my head and lip. There is a loud clang from the door.

"SHIT" hisses the locksmith, I ignore him.

"You know some Intelligence guys came up to me today and gave me a warning about my writing," I grumble recalling the event.

"What?" Lee stops her work for a second.

"Yup, apparently I'm on their list."

"Did they do this to you?" as if she could do something about it.

"No, this was the riot police and their fucking dogs." The antiseptic stuff stings my head.

"Those fucking dogs," it is the locksmith standing by the living room door, "you got a butter knife?" he asks rather embarrassed.

"Kitchen," I point.

Lee giggles,

"Is he fixing the door or fixing you lunch?" she whispers.

The locksmith walks back through the living room holding a butter knife and tugging at his shorts.

"Is this one okay?" he displays a dull, old butter knife that I've been meaning to get rid of.

"Perfect," I say, and he walks out to his station.

"You know in South Africa they had a problem after they canned Apartheid because the police dogs were still only biting Black people?" he yells from the door, "Those fucking dogs!" he ends with a sound of disgust.

"What are you going to do?" Lee asks.

"I'll have a beer. Worse things could happen." I am relaxed and comfortable.

"You know this is serious, right?"

"Worrying won't get you anywhere will it?" I remove my shirt to reveal the bruised shoulder. Lee gasps and grimaces. "Is it that bad?" I try to look at it but it hurts to turn my head that far.

"You need to quit these walks of yours. And I guess should have warned you about it, but that's why I didn't go to the varsity today." Her voice washes over me and gives me happiness. I close my eyes.

From the door I hear the locksmith venting,

"You know they threw people out of windows during the Boer regime. And those dogs ate *kaffirs* alive. Fucking canine squads and *chamboks*, secret police, tanks and guns shooting students." I begin to think that I should not have offered him that beer, but then I have an acute sense of the absurd, "The bloody humanity, I tell you! Those fucking dogs."

Lee giggles and rubs my shoulder. A while later, my wounds are taken care of and so is my door and I am a wad of bills poorer. The darkness is setting in. Who knows, tonight I may actually sleep. I begin to think about the warning I got. I guess those men were from the Central Intelligence Organization. The masses casually refer to them as the C-Tens. A joke has it that a new agent was being trained and was told that CIO stands for Secret Intelligence Organization, and when the initiate points out that secret begins with an "s", the trainer screams out that they are not paid to spell. I smile.

"You and John have a date tomorrow," Lee says.

"When was the last time *you* saw him?" I slur drowsily.

"That's not important."

"Why not?"

"Call him, you have to meet him at the Jazz Café." I have been smoothly disregarded.

"Great that's all I need, to hang out with a pile of anarchistic intellectuals and outspoken artists when I'm on the C-Tens' blacklist." I really just want to lie on her lap all day.

The setting sun paints the walls of the room orange and melancholy shadows of the window frames slither up the wall. It almost feels like I am drowning, as it gets darker and deeper in the room. My head feels lighter. Lee is watching a movie on the television. I lay my head on her thighs and step into the land of wakeful dreams. The room disappears about me as the universe created by my past fills the space. My breathing becomes softer and the pain of my body disappears. In moments my body disappears too. My eyes close from the outside, only to open to the disharmony of my ceremonial self and of temporal convention. I disappear inside of everything around me. It will be a while before I return. Who knows, tonight I may actually sleep.

Nodes of Night

Jeremiah and I walk out to the soccer fields outside the village school. It is the night of the full moon. A decent amount of cumulus clouds hover on the canvas of the night sky. The moon gives them a glow of luminous blue. The few stars that dare to challenge the brightness of the moon have earned their place.

It is celebration of the full moon, *jenaguru*. A teacher in high school always used to describe these celebrations to us. His focus of any ritual was the exploits of young couples behind trees and clumps of bushes. Of course, it being an all-boys Catholic boarding school, such descriptions were very welcome. There are many other people on the road. Young girls walk in groups and are better dressed than usual in their skirts and blouses. The boys are all in trousers and sandals. Many of the women have headed the way to set up the field.

Men join us and fling hearty pats on our backs. I am happy to be out of money now, as they would no doubt be hoping for me to subsidize another bout of boozing. Our skin is made a shiny navy blue by the moonlight, and all our clothing is shades of reds, browns and blues. Men energetically relay a stories about the events that ensued after our night of drinking at *Maraki's*. Apparently, one or two had befriended the night and slept in a ditch by the roadside. There had been one drunken brawl that ended in no injuries and drunken hug till the end. Thomas, who is walking between Jeremiah and myself, is half-drunk already and lets loose, in a stupidly loud, confidential whisper, that he had visited Maria, the local prostitute that all the men and boys have known (in more ways than one). But the top story that carries us all the way to the soccer field is that of Serio. The men say that he arrived at his compound and, in a fit of drunken idiocy, had tried to beat his wife, only to find *himself* fleeing the dwelling after his wife set him straight.

The field has no turf, nor any hope of ever having it, but it does have some sprouting *acacia* thorn bushes and treacherous stubs of dry elephant grass. Many soccer battles have been decided on this field by bare-chested boys, with enough adrenaline to make a herd of elephants have a seizure.

The field is full of people waiting for the dances to begin and the food to come out. The drummers warm their instruments at a fire close to ours. And the women bring out the first pots of beer.

A loud whistle signals the start of the action. A steady drumbeat colors the air and people gather. The young men of the village come out to dance. Their feet awaken the memories of the soil. They stab the air with sticks as they live out archaic motions of a hunt. Fathers applaud each other's sons. Mothers smile at the boys that are becoming men and the girls keep the song alive. They leap into the air turning and land on all fours. Whistles and roars flavor the performance as they sweat out a battle of agility and charisma.

The drummers sweat out the beat; their palms are hardened by the trance. There are three drums and men with clappers and shakers, and horns. The drummers carry out their own little performance as they somersault over their drums and back again, while drumming. They occasionally switch and take breaks to sip on the brews that are brought to them by the women.

The dust has not settled when it is the turn of the girls to contribute to this celebration of youth. Shakers are tied to their ankles. They stomp, throw their waists, and shake their shoulders. The saucier girls cast looks at the young men who watch with eyes bulging out of their skulls and gigantic grins moistened by saliva.

Jeremiah is talking with a loud group of men. I wander off to the drummers. I have lost my sandals somewhere. But the earth feels good on my soles. I take a seat with the musicians. They are having a joyous conversation. One of the older ones invites me to sit next to him by the fire. He seems familiar but I cannot put a name to his aged face. I recall him from my childhood, or maybe from one of *Ambuya's* stories. He snorts snuff from his palms and offers me some. I decline.

"Life is a long time," he says with wise laughter in his voice.

He lifts his horn and taps it twice on his knee then blows two raspy notes from it.

"It is to make the music pure," he says, "so that the music will not drown."

"Tell me," I ask, "what type of horn is that?"

He laughs,

"The type that sings."

He lifts the horn to his lips and begins to play. The music pushes through the air. Other musicians put their skills to work and add life to the old man's tune. The sounds find each other and quickly become a family. The man continues to play without raising his eyes like he is alone in the world he has conjured up. He stares at the fire so intently that it is hard to tell if the fire gives light to his eyes or if his eyes give life to the fire. I close my eyes and let the music heal and possess me.

In the backs of their minds were pieces of dreams pasted together by illusions. They all died a long time ago.

The drummers begin to add to the rhythm. I feel a bony nudge in my side, and the old man on the horn is beckoning me with head nods towards the drums. Before I can refuse, the lead drummer pushes the boy on the largest drum away from it. He looks at me with a large grin and nods me over. I am petrified. The drum looks large before me. The two other drummers are already submerged in the ocean of music and look to me to complete the sound. I place my hand on the drum and it is warm; this gives me comfort. I close my eyes to hear the sound of the other drums. I rub the skin of the drum and find myself smiling. My shoulders relax and my elbows become weighty. Raising my palm and dropping it in the center of the drum skin, I begin the journey into this world of sounds. I join in with simplest pattern. I can see that the other drummers are relieved.

"That's it *shasha*." The lead drummer encourages me.

I look across the fire at the old man with the horn. He is looking into the fire again and swaying slightly. People are beginning to dance around more. The alcohol is setting into most of the men and women. There is the fertile echo of ululation that carries us all to the next level. The other musicians surrender the celebration to the drummers and the horn as is traditional. My armpits sweat and my bare feet turn into roots. A warmth rises in me and I raise my face to the sky. The boy on the smallest drum has lifted it and is straying from the drum line and venturing into the crowd. He does not stop playing as he does this. His muscular legs carry him in a squat and throw him into a jumping turn that makes the women shriek and ululate. The men whistle and shout.

He leans up against one woman and she shakes her body to keep up with the beat. He finds this to be a challenge as the crowd laughs. So he puts the drum between his thighs and increases the pace to a frenzy. The woman refuses to be outdone and offers the him her vibrating rear. This becomes a signal and all the woman take up the motion. The lead drummer, beside me, catches on and lets out a whistle before switching rhythms. The people roar their approval, and I am pleased by my own fluid transition into the new beat. Gourds of alcohol are being passed over people's heads and over the fire. The lead drummer takes up a solo in which he uses an elbow and a foot then jumps over his drum once and shuffles back next to me. The people have stopped dancing and begun to clap. The fire is reflected in all their eyes, they clear the space in front of the fire and the stray drummer returns to the line-up. The empty space is filled with expectation. The lead drummer releases another solo, which he ends in a summersault, but before he lands, the relentless prodigal drummer jumps into a solo that is reminiscent of the shrill voice of a woman. And when he finishes, in accordance with expectation of the crowd, I take a leap of faith.

I forget where I am and let my palms do the talking. The big drum responds to the shrill drum and harangues it. The crowd laughs. The prodigal drummer returns and the little drum shouts at my drum. A comical conversation ensues between our drums much to the amusement of the crowd. The lead drummer switches the rhythm. My confidence is now in full swing. The horn lets out a single long blast that hushes the crowd as the drums continue. We now play for the ancestors. The lead drummer is stares into the deep unknown with unblinking eyes. The man on the little drum has fallen into a squat fully enveloping his drum. Warmth rises my ears. The music disappears from sound. Time becomes a lie. Nodes of night wash over me in grimacing waves of scorching desolation. I do not want to come back.

The sound of drums bursts back into my ears, and my eyes clear up to reveal an awed crowd, seated before the drummers. The old man lets out an obsequious blast from the horn, to appease the trance. He frees us. The moon is setting over the glade. The fire has turned to ash and there are some women caring for people who had "been visited". Things had happened, and they would be committed to the secrecy of the night and the prisons of memory. Women bring us beer and leave. We sit by the fire and drink, silently thanking those that moved through us.

Advent of Redemption

The lake of night pours waves of human fragrance over me as I am gathered together in a smoky corner of the café waiting for John. The space is already very much alive with the dancing of intoxicated, fit women to snappy afro-jazz rhythms. My eyes are drawn to one particular woman whose hips are swinging under her light, skirt. Her full lips shape an alluring grin. She is dancing in a group of four ladies, in front of the low platform on which a four-piece band is playing. Her friends are talking, dancing and laughing. But she is quiet, her eyes are with a mischievous silence. She looks at me and I recede into the shadows of the corner. Her brown shoulders are strong and she has a deep valley coursing down her back.

I lose my structure as a mirror as my palms move over the landscape of her body.

"Champion!" my trance is lifted and I land hard in the moment.

"What's kicking?" I lift my hand and slap John's palm.

"You look ok to me, man," he sounds loud to me, and indeed heads are turning in the café, "Lee made it sound like they had beat you senseless."

"Well…" I peek over at the dancing woman over John's shoulder as he sits down.

A clumsy but pretty waitress comes over, and I order John's *Zambezi* and another *Castle* for myself. On her way to the bar, another group flags her down, and she heads over to them. The room is filled with conversation. This is where the artists hang out. There is always something going on: poetry recitals, book discussions and bands playing. A lot of poets virtually reside here. The twelve odd metal garden tables are covered in beer mugs, glasses and bottles that the waitresses can only remove as fast as they are replaced. There is a lot of cigarette smoke, and the band is cloaked by a toxic haze. The lead guitarist is a skinny, average height fellow. Sweat drips from his forehead on to the floor. The black synthetic leather jacket shines oddly in the red and blue stage lights. He sways ands wiggles while bending his knees as he makes passionate love to his instrument. His face sets itself into a frown that ensures that the corners of his lips meet at his chin. The bass guitarist is motionless, like most bass players tend to be. He wears a cap, and his blue jeans are raised to his belly-button and fastened desperately by a thick black belt. The drummer floats in and out of jabbering fits in which he appears to be blabbering some tomfoolery along with the rhythm. The lead singer is a woman with a thick voice.

The Jazz Café is submerged in afro-jazz; the foreskin of reality folds back to expose our minds to the pleasure of time. The music tickles and taunts me as the rhythms shape themselves into a mockery that eludes me. With an odd smile, the plump little waitress places a whiskey in front of me. Maybe she is smiling at John who has spread before himself four bundles of cash that have appeared from his black leather jacket. He is engaged in loud conversation with the three men that have joined us. I am pleased to be relieved of the burden of having to carry conversation with John. My mind is on the music, the milieu and the river of words that flows persistently through my mind.

They surrounded us with visions of our own death; to ensure that there was not even hope. But in our minds, we replaced our faces with theirs. Our yells of pain became their cries for mercy. The death of our loved ones visions of the birth of a new nation. And in our soft, moist tears was a humid fertile song waiting to burst forth with the advent of redemption. Indeed they had guns on their side. But we had victory on ours. It rang out in our voices, followed us in our footsteps, and flowed in our sweat, blood and tears.

The band is quite a sight amidst a clutter of electrical wires and caged by fiscally retentive sound systems. The lead guitarist's fingers negotiate the convoluted frets of the neck of his guitar. They get tangled up in confusing twitches and convulsions that create beautiful music. The song they are playing now is fueled by blossoming lamentations on the improvidence of time. The singer's makeup is melting under her sweat. Her lips shape every syllable magnificently, and her deep voice makes the beer bottles on my table vibrate consentingly.

The dance floor is now occupied by six women who laugh as they dance. Through the fog of cigarette smoke and the haze of alcohol, they become nymph-like and dreamy. It is painless to fall in love during a dream. One of them keeps glancing in our direction, she's the one I was watching earlier. *She moves so easily all I could think of was sunlight*, I think that was Paul Simon.

As the song winds down to an end, she strolls over to our table and causes a pause to John's conversation. We all look up at her, and her eyes are trained on mine as she grins through shiny lips. Her braided hair is glistening. The buckle of her belt is a foot from my nose and I can smell her timid but flavorful perfume.

"Won't you introduce us, Champion?" John says to me.

"I would if I could."

"Julia," she says in a saturate intonation. It is like she is singing a line from a song.

The man next to me is already pulling up a seat between him and myself for the lady. She nods to him and sits down. Leaning suggestively close to me she says,

"I noticed you look at me, you look familiar," she is pulling out a cigarette pack, Marlboro Lights from her boots.

The conversation has revived itself among the other men.

"How about some fresh air?" She says.

"You want to get some fresh air while smoking a cigarette... true genius, I can't resist the offer." She laughs as she is getting up. I follow.

Before I know it, I am in the passenger seat of her brand new *Nissan Sentra* in the parking lot outside the bar. Through our zippers we explore our mutual access to each other and she is also kind enough to allow me access to her breasts by lifting her top adequately. After fifteen minutes of desperate grappling, thrusting and exploring her firmness, I emerge from the vehicle with bruises on my back from her long nails. We pull out our cigarettes as we walk back to the bar and she pulls out a lighter from her boots.

"What else do you keep in there?"

"Wanna see?" she lights herself and passes me the lighter.

"Whose car is that?" I ask.

"My husband's." I can't tell if she is being sarcastic. "How'd you bruise your lip?" she continues.

"Your husband." I am smiling and she laughs. "Thanks for the smoke," I say as I stub out my stick and open the door for her.

"Thank *you*," she says teasingly as she walks in.

She does not come back to the table to sit with me. Instead, she strolls over and joins her four friends at the bar. I notice her slide smoothly into the conversation, as though she was always there. I sit down and order another whisky. The three men are looking at me expectantly.

"Just a conversation," I lie and they return to their political discussion.

Turning to the bar I see her looking at me. She winks. We have kept a secret. The night drags on and I am completely inattentive to the conversation going on at the table. I keep my mind busy by watching Julia and her girlfriends as they return to command the dance floor. The musicians are playing nonstop and the bass player is looking red-eyed and sleepy. The drummer has a trickle of sweat running down his contoured face. The voice of the lead singer has become a part of my own mind, a part of me.

The greatest con is when you convince someone that you are them.

The song is a shaky rendition of a popular tune that has taken the urban radio stations by storm. The catchy lyrics and the impressive bass unite the generations in a celebration of amateurism and incompetence. It is quite a shift from the jazz they were playing, but it is a very welcome digression. A few drunk men finally stand to dance to this song and the ladies on the floor welcome them with their bodies. Julia is attacked by three zestful guys with drunken smiles. They are shaking their large stomachs at her. She tosses her head back and laughs openly. The shallow glimmer of her eyes flirts confidently. A dimple emerges on each cheek. The men sitting with us get up and stagger onto the dance floor.

"Will you dance, Champion!" John and I are left holding up the fort.

"Why don't *you* dance?"

"But your lady is on the floor."

"Where is yours?" I smile back at him.

There is a change in his face and he pulls his chair round to mine. Leaning forward he says,

"I'm not with Lee anymore, Champion," he gives me an earnest look that is void of sadness, "We're still friends but we're not ...you know."

I nod and pat his shoulder.

"No sweat, *ferrah*." I offer my condolences detachedly as we men do, and I order drinks for the two of us to appease the spirit of the deceased relationship.

The drinks arrive, two neat whiskies. John looks at me and the shadow of a beaten man flickers across his eyes for a split second. I pat his shoulder again and raise my glass. He follows suit. The burning gulp razes all his sorrow on its way down. Aware of the second part of the ritual, I raise myself to my feet and pull out my pack of cigarettes. John stands up and follows me out of the bar. And we stand by his car smoking. He inhales deeply.

"I'm not too stricken about the whole thing, Champion," he begins. "It actually feels alright, you know ... like the start of a new day."

I look at the stars in the sky as I take a drag.

"I can see that she didn't tell you, huh?" he smirks delicately.

"It's none of my business."

He is right she didn't tell me. But I am not really surprised or concerned. This always bugs people, my lack of concern. I wonder where Lee is right now. The stars are hard to see because of the glow of the street lamps. My cigarette is done so I toss it. John is still on his. I am of the opinion that there are very few things a man needs to say that cannot be said in the time it takes to smoke a single cigarette, hence the ritual. John will be fine. In fact he already is. His last exhalation is thick, smoky and cathartic. We walk back into the Jazz Café and the dance floor is still full. And the band has let loose another song by the same artist. I notice Julia glance at me as I follow John over to our seats. She is having fun. I smile as I sit down. She is strong. But I feel something inside me becoming taut like two worlds pulled apart.

The end of the night comes sooner than it should and I leave with my restrained lack of opinion. The chill is greater in the air, and sky is a little less than friendly. I feel like I should quit smoking as I place the cigarette in my mouth and light it up. I have never met anyone who's died of lung cancer yet. But my knuckles are chapped, and my shoulder hurts still. I do not want any part in this crazy life. As I say my goodbyes to John and the guys, my spirit throbs with an inexplicable anger. My car is cold and the door creaks when I open it. The dent shimmers in the orange slur of the streetlamp. I feel my chest burn suddenly as though conferring with the fact that my life is on fire. In a bid to make peace with my fury, I spit out the cigarette and exhale powerfully. The rage I should have felt during the riot begins to tick away like a time-bomb. I recall the line from a certain poet's piece, "I am the rape marked on the map/ the unpredictable savage set upon the page/ the obsequious laborer who will never be emperor." I turn on the ignition and drive home. I have much to resolve within myself.

Legionnaires and Lizards

The air rises with the sun in the morning. I sit like a lizard in the doorway of my room. Jeremiah's wives are going about their chores. And his second wife brings me some porridge in a bowl. The sun on her skin looks red. Our eyes do not meet. The wrapper she is wearing is the same one she wore two nights ago. As she is kneeling, she also places a large cup of water beside me. Her eyes, which are avoiding me, are the color of honey in the morning light. Many things about her seem softer and younger.

"I heard about your drumming," she catches me off guard.

Her eyes still stare at the ground. She shuffles back with a deliciously coy smile and leaves. I pull out the tobacco I borrowed from Jeremiah and begin to roll a cigarette. I recall the poem by Dudley Randall, "Black girl black girl/ lips curved as cherries/ full as grape bunches/ sweet as blackberries." I look at the dust before me and see Jeremiah's feet approaching. He sits beside me.

"It is morning," he sighs.

"Indeed."

"You are rolling for two, no?"

"Of course, though you may not be able to handle it," I smile.

"*The one who beats the drum*, who would have thought he came from the city, huh?" Jeremiah laughs.

I can imagine the shaping of fate. And that I will not be a part of it. Prison is the place for me. Nice and quiet. No one asks you questions or bothers you. Everyone is innocent, or so they say. The only truth is the pain inflicted by the wardens who are the messengers of all that is beyond the wall. And you can wonder what it is about freedom, this overrated freedom that makes them so angry as to offload their woes on our convicted backs.

"Jeremiah, did I ever tell you that I was jailed once?" My voice is trailing at a distance.

"Speak and we will hear," Jeremiah accepts the rolled cigarette.

I do not continue. I scoop up spoonfuls of the porridge. It is thick and sweet, mixed with peanut butter. As I do so I spot a group of six or so men with large sticks walking down the road and talking loudly. They wear white t-shirts with something written on them but I can't see what it is from this distance. One of them breaks off and walks into Jeremiah's compound. I can feel the air around Jeremiah grow heavy. The man is not wearing a white t-shirt like the rest. He has a red t-shirt with the face of Bob Marley stenciled onto it. The mob he is with has stopped at the entrance of the compound and is not coming in. The guy is young, maybe twenty or twenty-two. A bandana is wrapped in his scruffy hair. Pride is stamped all over his amble. As he stands over us I examine his cheap, paint-splattered jeans. I wonder if the splatter is a consequence of fashion or catastrophe. His nose is twitching oddly, probably meant to intimidate. There is a glazed fury in his eyes. I wonder what he wants with Jeremiah. But after a few seconds I realize what this may be.

"You are the writer, huh, from the city?" his voice is ridiculously high pitched, despite his clear attempt to make it deeper.

"Morning," I respond astounded.

"So you're visiting, huh. We do not want trouble, you see."

There is an awkward silence as I consider asking the boy about his jeans. He looks like he is fumbling for words being quite unaccustomed to such manner of response. Jeremiah keeps smoking with his eyes lowered. The young man continues,

"You see that my shirt is the color of blood, let us hope that none will be spilt while you are here," a nebulous threat.

I lean over to Jeremiah, completely ignoring the confrontational youth before us, and he gives me a light. Jeremiah laughs then sighs. I look over at the group standing around aimlessly by the entrance of the compound. I understand the situation. This event is a product of the times. Due to fear of the epidemic of radical thought, the administration must carry out purges. City folk are a threat in rural areas since they carry with them such diseases as educated opinion or worse yet, independent newspapers. But he called me "the writer". I guess this may be more than just the average check-up. They probably want to remind me that they are onto me. I suppose my renunciation of the profession is pertinent to their desires. I suppose the group sent the youngest one among them to do the talking, the rookie.

"When does the next bus come?" I ask.

"They don't scare you, do they?" Jeremiah asks.

"My brother, we used to beat up punks like these when we herded cattle back in the days. And we can still do it now,"

The boy in the red shirt is still standing before us as we ignore him. He shuffles a little, irresolute.

"You know, *shasha*, it always makes me smile how you appear not to care about anything," Jeremiah is still looking down, "*Nothing to lose*, heh?" he says in English.

Jeremiah and I used to be quite a team. No one could touch us. He was the colossus, and I was the headstrong blighter with behemoth rage. This little episode is reminding me of so many events of our youth. Our outright refusal to bend over for anyone. Of course it only got us into trouble back then. Big trouble. But we were always alive and together at the end of it. I can see where this is going as I feel the thunder inside Jeremiah growing louder.

"You remember those little bastards that time at the…" Jeremiah reads my thoughts and completes the phrase,

"The riverbed," and he laughs.

"We set them straight, huh? Five against two." I choke on cigarette smoke as I laugh.

Jeremiah's eyes become dangerous. He sucks in hard on his smoke and looks the youth in the eyes. His arms are over his knees and the veins are throbbing excitedly.

"Child," he says in a dark tone, "you come to *my* home, and do not greet me," he shifts his weight to sit more upright.

"Look, mister, I'm just…" the feeble lad begins shakily as he looks to his comrades at the entrance; they are oblivious to his situation.

"In front of my wives and children, and my visitors," Jeremiah's voice is now black as death, but to the stranger, it is nothing but a whisper.

I brace my self for action by pulling my legs in so I can rise quickly. I cannot help recalling that Bob Marley sang a song entitled *Zimbabwe*. Great song.

"If you want to cause trouble," the young man begins, but he does not finish.

In a single sharp stroke, Jeremiah kicks the chap's knee and there is a loud crack as the boy wails and falls to the ground. Landing hard he lets out a scream that I cut short with a punch

I land to his face as I get up. Looking up, I see that the mob has heard his wail and are yelling and stampeding towards us. I step on the boy's face as I go to meet them. Jari grabs my shoulder and shouts something as he puts something hard in my hand. It is a knobkerrie he pulled out of nowhere. My ears are burning, and I have lost my hearing: Symptoms of an adrenaline rush that I have not felt in a long time. Jeremiah also has a weapon. I cannot see what it is.

There are about eight of them and they are whistling and shouting with the sticks raised. For an instant I have a vision: A riot officer beating a fallen woman. I can smell blood in my nose. The mob advances but there are a few farther ahead than others. Jeremiah is two steps behind me. The first to get to me swings his large stick at my head as he is running. I dodge easily and side-step him. He goes by and I hear a tortured bellow of anguish, so I assume Jeremiah's had his way with him. The second dosser is slow to raise his stick. My knobkerrie lands squarely on his sternum. He falls over with his legs above his head and a bloody, gurgling gasp. Then the next two surprise me. One has a machete; blunt and rusty but it could still do some damage. It is raised and his red eyes are wide open. The dusty ground saves my life when I kick a root and fall right before the pair and the machete misses my head slightly. I land and bite the dust hard and the thugs trip over me and land harder.

Lying on my back I look back to see Jeremiah thumping the fallen blade-slingers in my wake. I raise my weapon to get up and hear a 'thunk' and my weapon shakes. Looking up I find a machete stuck in my club. I receive a kick in the ribs and I gasp. Three more venal youths are coming to join the beat down. With a labored swing I splinter the shins of the kicker and he falls onto me. I turn swiftly and end up on atop his chest pounding his face in with my left. My ribs file a mild protest that does not register. The three trailers are right above me with sticks and fists raised. Still sitting on my prey, I raise my hands realizing the end of my time is nigh. But a shadow flies over me with a shrieking whistle. It is an airborne Jeremiah. His head crashes in to the face of the lead hostile. The three of them collapse in a heap with Jeremiah on top whistling. The glorious chaos becomes lucid. As my hearing clears up I hear the growls of Jeremiah's two mangy dogs tearing at the clothing of the Mickey-Mouse legionnaires. I crash my club into the face of the semiconscious bungler I am sitting on.

In a bid to assist my friend a stick hits my back. It is a feeble strike, or maybe the natural painkillers are at work. I turn in a single swing and clout the offender unconscious. The war cries of the mob have turned into cries for mercy and apologies offered through toothless mouths and bleeding faces. The scruffy little mutts escort the limping botchers speedily out of the compound. I notice that Jeremiah has confiscated the machetes for his booty. A cut on the side of his head is bleeding mildly. On average, for both of us, more damage has been done to our clothing than anything else.

"You crazy son of a goat!" Jeremiah laughs as he slaps my shoulder.

"Your mother's a maggot..." I say swinging my arm over his broad shoulders.

"You remember the kids at the riverbed?" he yells.

"Yeah, they kicked our butts so bad,"

It is true, that the five-against-two childhood skirmish we mentioned was the day we returned home by riding our cattle. This is totally against custom, but we were beaten so badly by those kids we could barely walk. But we had fought, and we delivered our fair share of damage. We had fought. Today we have fought too. The sight we see when we turn to the compound and limp back exhausts our laughter. Jeremiah's wives and older daughters are screaming and wailing as though we are dead. The younger children are a range of emotions from petrified to entertained. In fact their yells have convened some support. Three of Jeremiah's neighbors had heard the commotion and scurried over the dry, dusty fields. They are carrying clubs and axes. They look abjectly alarmed. But they had missed the action. I let go of Jeremiah. And we both feign compunction to be appropriate.

After sitting for a long time in silence with the other men and having been served lunch, one of the men finally speaks up. He is the oldest of us, and of the chiefly lineage, which has been rendered practically impotent. But they are still respected.

"Jari," he begins "this is not good."

The group shuffles uncomfortably, Jeremiah keeps his eyes lowered. I follow suit. The group waits for the expedient rebuke which will comprise of three things: a chastisement of Jeremiah and myself for being violent and irresponsible, then an outline of things to be done to appease the amateur mercenaries, then the request for a public apology. But the elder surprises us all.

"If my bones allowed, I would have joined you," heads turn and look up at the old man, "They shall return though. For even a wasp always returns home after a battle to rest before it attacks again."

Everyone is silent like gazelles that have heard an ominous rustle in the bushes and can smell doom on the mental horizon. Fear is the most powerful chord of knowledge. And the old man has strummed it trenchantly. He is right; we had started something, now we must see it through.

Lavender Story, Bleeding Mahogany

My home is dark and hung with a damp loneliness. My door creaks open and I turn and lock the door behind me and make use of the second lock for the first time. It is still a little stiff since it's new. My breathing is soft and careful; I want to make it to my bed with out waking any of my sleeping turmoil. I walk slowly down the corridor and feel the still air on my face as a viscous fluid resisting my motion. My thoughts are heavy. I wonder why I carry them at all. Leaning against the wall, I slide down and sit with my back against the wall. The darkness of the passage clings to me like a tight shirt. It is soft. There is only the faint knowing light from the street lamp outside printed against the wall a few feet away from me by my bedroom door. My keys land with a morose and disrespectful jingle that disassembles the silence.

I spend a while seated there warming myself in the embers of emotions I thought I was no longer able to command. I write a letter to myself in my mind hoping that it will reach me sometime in the future. The letter tells me about the darkness of the present and how darkness is not always a bad thing. It is a letter of how night befriends me and wraps its cool wings around me and conceals me from the gaze of those that ride the backs of hyenas, the ghosts of my folktale past. How it shields me from all that could harm me. My letter to myself reminds me of things that used to make me smile and that I do not have to walk on my knees forever repenting, paying the debts of all those who have been sad. That I cannot bear the sorrows of all those around me. I am soft. As I pen out each rueful phrase in my mind, waves of truth and love wash over me fiercely. I can feel myself letting go of the island of who I was. My body begins to smile even though tears are forming on my face. I let myself go and I disappear.

From the distant caves of my inner refuge I hear my bedroom door open. It is Lee. The orange glow of the streetlamp reflects off the silky gown, which only goes down to her thighs. This has a sort of *deja* quality to it. She is barefoot.

"I couldn't sleep so I came over," her voice is soft and vulnerable. I can tell she has been crying.

"Hi."

Walking over to me, she sits before me giving me her shoulder. Her face hides in the nape of my neck. Her breath is warm. We sit on the cold floor together in the secrecy of the night. I tighten my hold around her shoulder and she sighs.

"I'm leaving," she says, "I'm going to my mother."

"Singapore?"

"Yeah," it is an inaudible whisper.

She immediately buries her face deeper in my neck as though apologizing. Her forehead is warm on my lips. I kiss it again and hold her tighter.

"And John…?"

She cuts me off by squeezing my shoulder and pulling herself closer to me. The night is cooler now. Holding Lee in my arms, happy that she is here at the end of my letter. I wonder when this letter will reach to me.

"I like it when you're here," I say.

Lee rubs the back of my neck. My eyes get watery so I close them. Warmth rises from my heart to my eyes. Her palm on my neck soothes with a soft caramel kindness. And I can smell her soft hair. She strokes my hair and kisses my forehead. Her neck smells like Himalayan rose, a smell I came to associate with happiness since I met Lee. Our bodies create a supple sculpture whose form relays tales of comfort in longing. Yearning aches and nostalgic anxieties. We become a single sullen structure held up only by a single, tired beam. Night shapes us into a desirable transgression of promise.

Slow as the first and dead at last. All in place and fluid, fluid as dark waters. Second movement slow yet quickened by the death of illusions. As I wiped your tears off my face and mine off yours. We glance at a fear seen only in the patterns of your dreams. Heads turn and we are seen for the first time in a new light.

In the third movement we embraced and knelt on the cold floor. Shoulders colder than ever. We had not been seen. The third movement was slow as the breath of the moment. We looked on as clouds darkened over the steeple. And in time with the hearts of wildness…we bled.

The puddle of blood grew around us as we disappeared in the fourth movement. Heads bowed down, we faded on our knees. The fourth movement was an eternity.

Making love to Lee is like carving. We twist and turn on the sheets grappling with an elusive necessity. The desperate heat of the moment and pleasant sourness as our bodies become organs of taste falls reluctantly. Lee sleeps holding me. I cannot sleep. I do not want to.

"Lee,"

"I know," she says and kisses me, "me too."

She falls asleep again. The light is encroaching. Yesterday came too soon. I recede into the land of sleep as I let go of the dream that I have just lived, carving memories into bleeding mahogany.

* * *

We wake up late in the afternoon and I roam the kitchen in my shorts with a bowl of cereal. Cereal is a bachelor's luxury. Since we have no time, or so we believe, to cook breakfast, we eat cereal. My body is light and I feel the cold air on my skin. Lee is in the bathtub. We have not spoken to each other at all. Our separate thoughts move us about the house. We are not avoiding each other at all. My lips curve into a jagged smile, it is almost like we have been living together forever. I toss the empty bowl into the sink and it lands with a clang. Standing before the sink, I look out the window and see the locksmith's children playing in the street with wire-frame cars. The cars are skillfully made from rusty bits of wire foraged in obscure crevices of the cityscape. I remember playing with one or two such models in my younger days. I stand there scratching my head watching the children and pondering this celebration of high-density residential urbanity. The children are barefoot on the tarmac. One chap is topless and therefore exhibiting his ribcage and large stomach. The other lad is smaller and struggling to keep up with his older brother. The shirt he wears is unbuttoned and flailing about behind him and his protruding, abstruse bellybutton. The wheels of the cars are old battered shoe-polish tin cans. Long sticks act as the faulty steering mechanisms of the contraptions. Those toys actually look safer to be in than some of the public transport that's on the roads. I laugh out loud and stretch sleepily curving back and reaching up to the ceiling.

"Someone's happy this morning." It is Lee standing by the door in my red shirt.

"Morning," I chime, "you know the kitchen better than I do, so help yourself."

"Um-hm,"

"I could use a bath myself," I say as I walk past her to the bathroom.

She brushes shoulders with me deliberately and pushes me off balance.

"You just want to start a fight, don't you?" I joke as I hug her and give her a little shake. She giggles.

As I close the bathroom door, she yells,

"We're going shopping,"

I open the door and stick my head out,

"You think that writers have all the time in the world, don't you?" I feign annoyance, "I'm a very busy man, Lee."

"Yeah, right."

After my bath, I'm ready to go. Lee is standing by the car and I emerge with a twenty-five liter container of petrol. I place it on the bonnet of the car and push a piece of hose into it.

"Where'd you get that?"

"Secret stash," I say slyly as I kneel by the car tank and begin to suck on the hose.

"I don't know how you do that," she says clearly repulsed.

Quickly, I pull the hose out of my mouth and into the car tank. I spit a little petrol out of my mouth and wipe my lips with the back of my hand. The siphoning has begun.

"I don't like waiting in the queues,"

"Doesn't it taste bad?" she asks with girlish concern on her brow.

"I don't know, why don't you try some," I pretend to offer her the hose and she screams.

We are living in the times when "Black is beautiful" is more in reference to the black market than the race. Our indulgence in this blackness unites us all. Lee is not quite awake to this Zimbabwe yet. It is like the Tale of Two Cities. She lives in the other one where black market fuel is a distant myth, and the only inconvenience is the fact that she'll soon need a wheelbarrow to carry all her money. Sometimes I think of her as the lead character in Paul Simon's song *Diamonds on the Soles of Her Shoes*, and this is the part of the song where "she makes the sign of a teaspoon," and "he makes the sign of a wave."

The vegetable market is in the part of the city that, in colonial times was the bosses' dumping ground for expired negritude. There are tenements with rooms that are fifty square feet large. There are five or six families in each of these dark windowless spaces with the only barrier between them a moth-eaten curtain. There are roads in the potholes as opposed to potholes in the roads. It is the promised land for litter and garbage. Here, dirt and litter can roam free, sit, mould and decompose undisturbed. I always tense up when I come here as I'm sure rich people do when they come to my neighborhood.

Lee is dressed impeccably as always and I am dressed well, same as always. We park my car outside the walled market and enter the world of the vending, loitering and good vegetables, that is, cheap vegetables. A welcoming committee of filthy teenage boys dressed in torn and ragged clothing approaches and engulfs us in an ill-odored reception.

"Just a twenty, *shasha*, and your car is safe," says one boy.

Some are closing in on Lee, but she stays composed and tells them to talk to me. I scan the mob, and find the most intimidating looking chap who looks like he runs the crowd. The guy looks drunk and high. His hair is twisted. And he has a cigarette in his mouth. His half-closed eyes show that he is a derelict bastard who doesn't give a fuck about anything especially not my car.

"You," I say pointing at him and pulling out a bill with nine zeros, "be good to it, champion and I'll give you the rest when I get back."

"No sweat, *biggaz*." He swipes the note from my hand.

The rest of the mob is pissed off and they walk away complaining.

The market is dense and humid, filled with all manner of vegetables at all manners of prices. I always want to leave as soon as possible when I come here. But Lee wants to touch smell and sample everything twice before she even starts to bargain. Then she walks around many more times before she considers buying anything. So I space out and follow like a mindless troll making sure no one bugs her. I even carry her handbag for her. The vendors are an interesting mob that ranges from the ones that coerce you to the ones who act as though they don't need your money and treat you like dirt even though you're the customer. But Lee is a master in the psychology of the market. By the time we leave we have a decent stash of vegetables for a decent price and my car is safe.

"Why'd you pick that guy for the car?" Lee asks casually.

"Coz he doesn't give a fuck about my car, but he wants to get high quick," and I add matter-of-factly, "And he'd kill any-one of those other guys for that money."

"Hmm…"

I roll down the window and put my hand out to feel the wind. We drive alongside a fuel queue with men sleeping in their cars or reading newspapers or chatting leaning against their vehicles.

"I'm leaving you my house," says Lee suddenly. I listen, "You can rent yours out and live in mine so you'll have some income"

"Lee…" I begin.

"And I'll have somewhere to stay when I visit. And you can always move back to your house when I come back and kick you out," her voice is painfully convivial, " It's all set up, you just have to sign a deed." She is serious.

My heart kicks my chest once, hard. The wind feels a little cold on my arm. We pull to a stop at a traffic light. I squeeze the gear lever and Lee puts her soft palm over my hand and strokes it gently. I look over at her and see that she is looking out her window. I cannot see her face, but I can feel the lavender palm writing a story on the back of my right hand. The same hand I used to wipe the black market fuel off my lips. I lift my hand with hers on it, and I kiss her hand. The light turns green, so we go.

Zindoga

"Outside the Village, there lived a man. He had lived there for a while. That was long ago. No one lives there anymore. The land the man once lived on was now overgrown. The Forest had been taking it back slowly. The man would never come back; he was on a journey. The expedition would end in his death, he did not know this, and he did not care. He was looking for his Bird. She had left him, or rather he had set her free." We shuffle and readily inhale this fragment of a tale, knowing that it will all make sense later.

I am still curious about what happened to the Daughter and the plague in the Village. But I trust *Ambuya* will not forget.

"This man had lived all alone on his land surrounded by the forest. He was a farmer, a large man. He was twice the size of a big man. To encounter his enormity on the forest path was a rarity. Silence was the sound of his footsteps, and his breathing was like the wind. His hair was twisted and knotted into dejected dreads that rolled past at his shoulders. The children started a rumor that he was the one that stood in the glade between this world and that of the ancestors. Some even made it a challenge to see who could find where he lived in the forest, but none ever did. Only the Oracle knew where he lived and the decaying wretch had no reason to let anyone else know. This man had been called once a long time ago to help the Village kill a lion that had eaten some cattle. He refused so the elders ostracized him. This was ridiculous since he had never had anything to do with the village for as long as anyone could recall. He lived alone farming and hunting. Few from the Village ever saw him. To some he was a myth, like the Reed Flute Traveler. He had been there for a long time. People had forgotten why he did not live in the village, but some say it was because he killed a man. They were wrong - he had killed many, but it was not of his willing.

"The Weaver heard the news of the end of the plague and the celebration feast. He summoned his wife and told her of the feast. She said she had heard and was already preparing their contribution. The Village was alive with activity. Little children ran rampant, as they capitalized on their mothers' distraction. Hens and roosters ran unbridled, carrying out sordid acts in the most public places they could find. The day progressed and the Weaver went about his business quietly. He thought of how his daughter would have enjoyed the preparations. Then he stopped himself and fought back a tear. *He must not cry.* His wives had done well in restraining the tears accordingly, believing that the Daughter would return. Her mother had retreated deep within herself and buried her daughter there. Her tears were well stored. For all this time she went about her work, as though her daughter was at the river. Or maybe she had forgotten to remember."

Sentinels of Thought

Walking again down the street, I see the face of a mod-ern-day hero. The posters are lined up against the wall form-ing a train of peculiar hope. The face on the posters is that of the singer of dangerous songs. The one who had chosen to stand before an angry rooster unflinching. The face has gener-ous, stern lips and large nostrils breathing fire. A light moss-like covering of beard, purposeful slick brows and sober eyes. Healthy dreadlocks claw out at the observer like guardians of his thoughts. There is something very iconic about the posture, like a Russian Bolshevik. This is the face on the wall. You will only see this poster in large cities. This is where truth-tellers may still show their faces on occasion. Their features may only appear like the glimmer of moonlight on a lake at night, fleet-ing, obscure and only suggestive.

The posters are for parliamentary elections. The instruc-tions say to vote for this revolutionary on the given date. The date expired a long time ago. The posters are faded and some are torn. Some have random obscenities graffitied all over them. In a vulgar instant, the ten meters of wall become a postmodern comment on the hopes of a generation with frayed ends. Our hopes rise and fall like a scummy tide. We sit and wait for po-litical messiahs. We wait with a festering heart. Each citizen becomes a groaning pillar in the cathedral of ineffectual prayer.

Be quiet, my soul for God knows the time and shall do his willing, and give you rest.

My publisher wanted to have a word with me, so I had strolled into town. I stared at his tobacco-stained teeth for an hour. I have no idea what he was talking about, but it is done. I mentioned my run-in with the feds and he offered me help if I wanted to run away. He said he could send me just about anywhere in the world. I thought of Singapore. He laughed and asked why on earth I would want to go there. He said it was possible, though. But I do not want to go anywhere. My work is getting published, I have no idea why.

I turn into a little store and head for the liquor section. The security guard sits sleepily by the door on a metal frame which I guess I should take for a chair. The cool dimness of the store is welcome. Many shelves are empty and dusty. But the liquor section is full. The more expensive bottles are dusty. They are higher up on the shelf. I bend over and pick up a little bottle of Chateau brandy, my poison of choice. I smile at the sad fact that perhaps some of the few choices people have are only concerning the type of alcohol to buy. I get to the counter. And pull out the advance I got from my publisher.

"This one's on me," sings a voice.

I turn and see Julia behind me.

"Are you stalking me?" somehow I am not surprised.

"Only if you want me to be," she slaps a note on the counter.

The bored and livid teller picks it up and punches in the numbers. I pick up the bottle and thank her as I stuff the bottle in the back of my pants.

"So how about lunch?" says Julia.

"Who's paying?" and we walk out of the shop.

The fast food place is unfamiliar to me. But it looks like Julia is a regular. She greets the staff casually. We sit for a long time and eat. I spike my soda with brandy and Julia laughs. As we speak I think of the words of a certain deranged genius writer. It was a particularly wonderful flow about language. Sitting opposite Julia, I "rub my language against" hers and it is soothing on the skin of my mind.

"You don't have anywhere you need to be?" I ask noticing the time.

"Do you?" she is scribbling on a piece of paper.

She slides it over to me. It is a telephone number.

"Is this your husband's number?"

"Maybe."

I take her pen and scribble my number on the other side of the paper and slide it back to her.

"Just to be safe," I say.

"Smart man," she says picking up the paper.

"Nope, just lazy…"

I get back on the road. Taking swigs of the brandy as I go. It is a good thing I bumped into Julia, I probably would have had another hunger-strike day. The brandy goes down better after the meal anyway. I walk into the park and sit on a park bench in the humid shade. Leaning back, I throw my arms over the back of the bench and slouch. The brandy bottle is in my right hand. People walk by and look at me. They probably think that I am some besotted sloth who has fallen onto the wayside of life. Perhaps they are right, I do feel awfully fatigued.

Last night after going to the market, I had driven Lee home. And we walked into her house. I was shocked to see three large bags already packed beside the door. She did not look at me. I followed her into the dining room and the papers for the house were on the table. I signed the papers and Lee enveloped a copy, called in one of her workers and told them where to post the envelope. I left the room and went to sit out on the back porch. My eyes looked about my new property. I heard Lee come up behind me. She touched my shoulders.

"When?" I asked.

"Early morning. Midnight flight." Her voice was shaky.

She broke down and I held her. I drove her to the airport, and she left. We had made love once more, desperately. She was burning inside and her tears were steaming. I held her. Now she is gone. The bench is warm on my back.

I suddenly feel that my firmament has shrunken. Emptying out the bottle, I rise and go home. I take my computer and clothes, and pile them up into the car. Collecting a few more valuables, I head over to my new residence. I drive off into the sunset, across the poverty line, uninspired and unexcited.

I am night and dreams taste good on my tongue.

* * *

Sleep runs from me as though I am Death. I wrestle with my sheets. The bed is large, foreign and cold. The ceiling looks unfriendly. And the walls play a game with my mind by moving up and down. This is the room Lee used to spend her nights in. This is the bed we consecrated twice with our love. And in those worshipful nights we had grappled and writhed in sheets she had twisted into ropes with her soft palms. Sheets moist with love. I just wanted her to stay. To run her river of love over me like a goddess. To kiss my broken wings so I can lift myself again. But it is too late to think of that now.

I sigh and roll to the edge of the bed. Sitting up I reach out for my packet of cigarettes on the bedside table. I put on a t-shirt violently and walk out to the veranda. The floor is cold on my naked feet. Naked- an interesting word. It hints at utter spiritual and emotional desolation accompanied with physical unclothed-ness. As opposed to Nude, which would imply collaboration between subject and artist. My feet are naked. This chain of thought carries me to the room I used to sleep in when I used to visit Lee. It is now a study. I moved a little desk in from another room. And placed my laptop on it. I toss the pack of smokes on the bed and sit to write.

As my body seats itself, my mind moves to Jeremiah like a memory of sadness. I feel like life is a dream I have been slowly letting go of. Blessed are the meek, beaten, trampled and spat upon. Only allow your honor to be pimped and you shall enter the kingdom. *But who will hold my hand as I slip away.* I have been told that Fear, apart from being a very useful human response, is one of the most illogical. I have also been told that "too much fear breeds misery in the land." My fears swirl in the porridge of festering hope and unclear, acute responsibilities. They bound and leap in clamorous insistences that shape my cage of open air.

And as though confirming my fear, there is a knock on the main door. I freeze and a sharp stab rushes through my chest. My heart beats loudly. At this hour, there is very little else that could be the matter. In my head I hear a voice that sounds familiar saying: *They have come for us.* It is true; I am many people all in one. I choose an ambassador for this situation. Walking to the door, I see my life prematurely flash before my eyes. I am dizzy. My eyes begin to well up with tears. This is a terrible way to go. To disappear in the night, alone. I get to the door and stand behind it for a second.

"Who is it?" My throat suddenly becomes dry.

My voice is hoarse and my legs are unreliable. My ears begin to burn as I await the response. My time has come.

"It's me sir, my wife is unwell," my relief is ridiculous.

It is the worker's feeble voice. He sounds desperate. I feel a tickle in my ribs, and almost laugh. Unlocking the door, I see him standing there looking afraid.

"Sorry, sir, but I think she needs to go to hospital," he is shaking, "I don't know what to do."

"Don't worry," I say and run back in to get dressed.

I get outside to the car and see him struggling to move the feeble skinny lady. I go and assist him. She is cold and sweating. We exit the high gate and the guard lets us out once we have woken him up from a juicy sleep. He is wrapped in a thick navy green coat and a scarf. He doesn't even appear embarrassed in the least. I will relieve him of his duties soon due to his vocational impotence.

"Take care of the house, we'll be back,"

"Ehh…" he says, red-eyed and yawning.

As we drive to the hospital, I finally get to spend time with the two people who had spent their entire lives in service. Lee has said that they had raised her pretty much. I look and see that the man is maybe in his mid-forties and is known to me only as *Mukoma*, which means big brother (though he is more like an uncle in age). His chin has about two days worth of beard. And it is graying. There are deep furrows from the corners of his nostrils to the corners of his lips. His look is greatly concerned. I had told Lee not to worry about them when she left. So since today, they are my employees, even though I have no idea what to make them do for me. I guess they'll make my meals or something. I had only had a few conversations with the man in the past. Short and polite dialogues about the weather and stuff. Lee had explained the situation to the man. Apparently his wife did not really work for Lee, she had been a vendor. She grew vegetables in Lee's garden and sold it on street corners. But that had become impossible, so she was unemployed.

"She had complained of a headache earlier," he says, "Then tonight I saw that things were not well with her, so I thought I would take her tomorrow. But in these early hours, things turned for the worse. I'm sorry to disturb."

"Don't worry, *mukoma*," I say, "I was awake, it is no problem."

We arrive at the hospital and park in the lot closest to the emergency room. The lights are stupidly bright inside. We bring her in and place her on a wheel chair. The nurse is unusually chipper. I greet her and explain the situation. Another nurse comes in and he is the quiet sort. The room is large and there are three or four groaning people seated in the hallway. I look at them. The reception nurse follows my gaze and decides to get to the next stage.

"After the forms are filled, there will be need for a twelve-million dollar payment before she can see the doctor. If she needs to spend the night, there will the need for another six million dollars." She says it in a tone that hints understanding.

Mukoma, beside me, moans a little and shakes his head. He moves slowly for his ragged pouch, which clearly has no such amount of money. I quickly say,

"No problem," and my hands move quickly and slap a few bundles of money on the counter.

The reception lady nods at the male nurse who was standing like a medical sentinel. He takes the bundle of illness in the wheelchair and rolls her down the insanely bright corridor past the groaning patients who I presume were unable to pay the bill just yet so we got priority. It's a good thing I had gotten that advance earlier today. I just hope the work sells well.

"You should go with her, *mukoma*," I suggest.

"Thank you, sir," he is struggling, "the money…"

"We'll talk later, don't worry."

As he goes off after his wife I think to myself that I should start seeing about renting out my old house or else I'll be dead broke soon. I could have the locksmith help me take care of that. I stick around and fill in the forms on the counter.

"That was very nice of you," says the nurse.

"It must be hard working here,"

"Hm…" she nods and turns away.

The brightness of the lights exposes all the flaws of the hospital. People's suffering is illuminated. Poverty manifests itself in the form of people unable to pay to save their lives. I assume because of the transport problem some may be dying in their homes at this moment since you would have to sell your leg and child to afford an ambulance anyway. The hard metal benches stare at me. The air is cold and thick in the room. I leave out *mukoma's* name on all the forms, as I don't know what it is. I sit and wait. After fifteen minutes, I see a doctor walking down the hall with my employee. As he introduces himself, he seems tired.

"It is a mild case of anemia caused by malnourishment, I assume. Her immune system is giving in." Then he lowers his tone slightly, "Judging from her description of her lifestyle, there is little to be worried about, we'll do a few tests." He nods a little, looking me in the eye.

"Malnourishment?"

"Times are tough, sir." He says then changes subject, "She will need a pint or so of blood, she should be fine. But it may take a while to find the blood. She can stay here till then if finances allow, and I do advise it."

"Thank you," I say.

The doctor leaves and I stand there with *mukoma*.

"She needs blood." He sounds distant.

"Yes," I say, "It's no problem."

I walk over to the reception desk and unload a few more bundles of money. After completing the forms *mukoma* looks distraught. I decide to ease his mind. Knowing that he will not be at ease with charity, I tell him that I'll take five percent of his wages every month till the debt is repaid. I do not tell him that I am giving him a raise. After he has said goodnight to his wife, we drive home. I am silent. And I can tell he is a little embarrassed. He and his wife had been starving quietly behind the main house in Lee's presence and did not have the heart to ask for a raise. And Lee, blissfully naïve Lee, had not noticed. I turn to him explaining that now that he works for me some things will have to change, well mostly one thing: When he buys food for the house, he shall always buy enough for three people; he and his wife shall eat the same as I do.

The hospital's hunt for blood may take a while, two or three days if we are lucky. As we near the mansion, my thoughts return to my response to the knock on my door. My fear. How could I have been so afraid? Am I another one of the sheep with predetermined responses to the law enforcers? I lay my fear before me, naked in my mind. And I am embarrassed. On arriving, I enter the house and lie in the large bed awake. My fears dance around me and taunt me. I try to understand them as the soiled faction of my being. They reach out and stroke me and I recoil desperately. But they stay close. My sleep is laborious and slack.

But who will hold my hand?

* * *

Buried in the Sky

The next day hangs on our shoulders like a hoe at the end of a long day in the fields. The sun is bland, it shines effortlessly and uncaringly. Jeremiah and I sit about the household doing nothing. As I scratch my chin, I am happy to find it with a few days' worth of unshaven growth. I have not shaved since I came here. My body aches a little from the fracas of yesterday's rumble. But my spirit is rejuvenated. Our refusal to share our nest with the thugs had spread in the village. But no one has dared to visit us. The people are afraid to be seen associating with us. I am happy to have fought. The consequences we face include losing a few acquaintances. Time is measured in a steady flow of cheap cigarettes as we await the next challenge. Jeremiah has no work today. He is looking down into the sand and marking it with a stick. He is drawing lines then erasing them. Making intricate patterns that mirror the events of his mind I suppose. I look up and see one of his little sons herding cattle out of the kraal and off into the meadows. He is joined by a boy and his herd on the dirt road. They are chattering excitedly as they mark the dust with little stories of their feet. Their footprints mix with those of the cattle. I smile.

The rays seep lackadaisically into my skin. I know I will be darker by the time I get back to the city. The city. My thoughts back away from it. I am glad to forget about the city for a while.

Getting up from the ground, I dust my pants. Jeremiah looks up at me and begins to speak then hesitates. He looks down again and begins to draw in the dust. The sand rushes away from the stick as it passes through. It gives way to the scrolling. Its magically damp, golden color jumps and skips with a poetic scraping sound of unrefined finesse. Staring at it I recall a childhood spent in the mazes of the mind. When all around me served as food for my imagination tree. It had grown tall and strong. Then the sharp-toothed saws of pedagogy felled it down.

"Where to, my brother?" Jeremiah sighs.

"The mountain."

"The mountain?" he has looked up.

"*Ehe*, don't worry, I shall return."

I go into the kitchen. It is amazingly dark inside. The thatched roof is black with soot. I am startled by a stupid hen that squawks and runs between my legs on its way out. I had caught it digging into the torn sack of maize-meal. The water tastes a little like rusty metal. It is thick and sharp on my tongue. There is the sound of talking outside so I return to see. It is Jeremiah and his first wife speaking. She is seated with her legs folded under her. She speaks respectfully with a low tone. Her voice is dull and deep, but calming. She is taller than the second wife and she has a fuller build. Her hair is wrapped solidly and her back is curved at the shoulders. She gets up and leaves. I walk up to Jeremiah.

"Serio's brother is lost to us," he announces the death calmly "We shall go to their home in the evening. He will be buried in the morning tomorrow."

"How?"

Jeremiah waits a little then,

"In these times who is to know? Darkness falls upon everyone. He had gone to the city and worked for a bit then returned. He had been ill for a while," he said.

This is the way *the disease* is narrated. The story is all too familiar. Death is all too familiar. Normalcy. There had been a time, I'm sure, when people would cry and weep and be shocked with each death. Now we all just hope there will be someone to bury us when we die. There is no wisdom in living for too long, they say, for who shall bury you if you are the only one left?

"People are dying like cattle in a draught," Jeremiah makes a sound of disgust and shakes his head, "every week we must dig a new grave. We shall soon fill the earth and have to bury people in the sky."

I make respectful sounds of agreement from the hollow of my chest. My eyes look to the ground.

"When I die you should burn me," Jeremiah sighs.

"Your wives will kill me before they allow that to happen. They will remove my testicles and feed them to your dogs. "

"Just as well, *shasha*, they need some food."

"A good way to die," I venture, "would be like that girl in *Ambuya's* tale. To drown and have a stranger of kindness waiting for you at the bottom."

"That's a shit way to go, man," Jeremiah takes the bait, "to have no one know where you were or how you died."

"But is dying not personal? Who should know where and how if they are not dying with you? For even a dog goes to find a secret place to die. My death is my own."

"Are you saying you want to die alone? What about those who care for you?"

"As with the story we were told, they will find ways of appeasing their selfish love for you," I say.

"But the Basket Weaver set out looking for his Daughter, no?" Jeremiah has dropped his stick to the ground.

"That was only because he took up the side of the big guy in that fight when they tore up the village. They each went for their own selfish reasons."

"My brother, it's a terrible thing to die alone. They do not need to die with you. But it is good to know that you are not alone like a large rock in the middle of a lake that goes on till kingdom come. It is not good to die alone." He sounds as though he has died once before – alone.

His voice is expansive and heavy with truth. I rest my case. I have understood his words in a place deep within my self. The afternoon glides past quickly as we are seated outside. We occasionally get up to follow the shadow of the little mango tree. I get one of the children to bring me a mat and I lie down on it under the warm blanket of air beneath the tree. The occasional buzzing of wasp wings taunts my ears but I am soon asleep in a pool of shallow breath.

* * *

"The *Zindoga* grabbed grown men and threw them through compound walls. They came out with their arrows to kill him but he simply caught them before they left the bow. With large logs he demolished the huts of the village. The women and children watched helplessly while the men fought in vain." Her voice was as excited as it had ever been and we sat wide-eyed, the horror taking form in our imaginations.

"They finally managed to catch him with many ropes and tied him down. As they awaited the elders' decision, the strangest thing happened."

"What happened?" squeals a little toddler who we forgive lest the tale never be completed.

"The Oracle came and told the Basket Weaver to free the large man and walk with him."

"Why?"

"Shhh!"

"Well," whispers *Ambuya* with raised arms, "to find his daughter. He was to walk with the loner in the forest. The Weaver needed to know no more, he took his blade and cut the ropes that tied the man down. Together they fled the Village leaving behind a shower of arrows and spears. And so began their journey, one they would complete with out speaking a single word. Not one. One looked for his bird, the other for his daughter. And you know, the forest is a dangerous place."

Our eyes are still glazed and thirsting when we are told to go to sleep. The night air greets us with familiarity, strange though it is to us. Our soles print mingled sentences in the dust.

* * *

We arrive at the funeral late at night. There is no need to rush to death, Jeremiah had said when his wives suggested they leave earlier, death will catch you soon enough. At least a hundred people fill the yard. Whimpering can be heard from the room that is designated for the women. They sniffle and moan tearlessly. This is only the beginning. The virtuosos in this field know to save their true wailing for the hours when it is most inconvenient for those that are nodding off. Jeremiah and I shuffle in to the compound and immediately fall silent. Many hands are held and many backs patted. I recognize the silhouettes of many strangers as I offer my condolences. And they accept without knowing who I am. The darkness blends all our sorrows into a sublime orgy of mourning. Purple tears and rune-shaped frowns are revealed by the occasional flicker of dim lamps and dark flames.

"These are the hardships we face," I intone with each interaction.

"We have seen them," or "they have been seen," respond the people.

This is how we ignite each other's pain, and by the touching of the skin on our palms, we acknowledge our humanity and weakness in the face of death. Jari and I find our way to the fire with the men and the elders. Serio is seated on an archaic couch, and everyone is seated about him silent and respectful. It is a bastardized portrait of the Last Supper in which the knock-off savior, seated in the center, is unable to raise anyone from the dead. And the disciples lack the energy and discipline to be animated or heavenly in any way. An old man releases a phlegm-textured cough. The fire reveals him to be wearing an old dress hat with the spine of a feather stuck in it and a waistcoat under his suit jacket. His eyes are cloaked by the deep shadow of his hat. There are about twenty men around this large fire. Jeremiah and I walk about greeting each man allowing each handshake to linger appropriately. Some of the men color the interaction with a shake of the head or a sigh. Serio looks up to see who it is that is consoling him. Recognizing us, he sighs and lifts his hand.

"Only yesterday we danced together at Maraki's, now death has claimed my brother! Who would have known?" his voice is tortured but his eyes are dry.

"None could have known, my friend," Jeremiah pats his shoulder.

As we seat ourselves on the smoky side of the fire, we hear the women in the hut raise their voices in a chaotic hymn. Their voices are coarse as they splatter sound into the night like paint on the canvas of an abstract painting. The shakers and drums are distraught and almost penitential. The night is startled awake again. This song also creates space for more wailing. And as if on cue, a large lorry with at least thirty people in it pulls into the compound. They are singing their own hymn to announce their arrival. They must be from the city. I can tell because their hymn is more refined and lacking in the ardent vernacular of the other women. The event rises to a frenzy in which the city hymn is taken up by the women leaving the hut to greet the newcomers. Women's voices are raised pathetically to the heavens. It is hard to tell the true mourning from the false. The men remain seated around the fire. Serio whispers into Jeremiah's ear, at which Jeremiah signals me to follow him.

"We must see to the skinning of the bull, and get the boys to do it."

I nod my head and follow. Behind the kitchen is a frenzy of activity with women in wrappers preparing food. Young girls are laughing restrainedly as they converse. And a few young boys are gathered about a decapitated bull with bloodied hands and clothes. Jeremiah does not waste time.

"Go tell the women we need knives, many of them. And you must sharpen them before you bring them back." The boys seem to know him. To another he says,

"Go get large dishes and a wheel barrow, to put the meat in after we cut it."

"No problem, Mukoma Jari." He runs off.

The bull is clearly very dead. It looks like an obscure mound in the darkness.

"We need light," I say.

"You," Jeremiah points at a youngster running by, "tell the driver of the lorry to bring it round here, tell him we need light to skin the bull." The reluctant fellow scurries off.

In a few minutes the loud lorry pulls up round the hut and parks before the meat and turns on its headlights. The black bull is illuminated. The head lies a few centimeters from the front of the body. Its eyes are half open and its tongue is hanging down into the sand. Half the body is caked in sand and blood. The boys bring the blades and the dishes also arrive. A few more boys gather. Jeremiah takes a knife and I follow suit. He cuts the skin down the belly of the bull and I cut the incisions on the inside of the front legs. Then with small cuts and digging with the handles of the knives, we begin to remove the hide from the fatty flesh. The carcass is still warm and smells like a butchery once it is open. We surround the sacrifice and strip it naked with our knives. Jeremiah monitors the progress to ensure the leather is not damaged. The tools are blunt and require constant sharpening. The young men assisting us talk about how the meat will taste good and how certain people are to be kept away from the meat. Sadness creeps into me and I find myself apologizing to the dead bull as I skin it. I am gentle but skilful with my blade.

When skin is removed, Jeremiah proceeds to disembowel the bull. As steam rises from the belly of the bull, new and unpleasant odors are born to the air. It is strange how the death of one causes that of another. The piteous fate of livestock: to become a sacrifice fed to hordes that gather to mock the departed with their forced tears. To be the one to appease the hunger of another with your life. To have them feast on your body and blood and not even know your name. You will only be remembered by the piece of leather you leave behind that will be given to one of the elders of the family. Jeremiah assigns hacking of the flesh to the husband of Serio's younger sister. As I wash my hands of the blood, the sounds of singing from the women agitates a memory of a death and a funeral. I was only a child. My pants smell like the flesh and blood of a bull. My heart is heavy. My head throbs suddenly as though fighting a thought. The night becomes thicker and cooler. The memory becomes more real. I was only a child.

* * *

Barbwire Lullaby

"Champion, you know, I've heard things." John looks a tad concerned.

"What sort of things?"

"I have friends in interesting places, you probably know." His smile is false.

"Go on."

"You may be in some trouble if you're not careful. I've told them not to worry. That you are just another rambling fool. But I don't know if they believe me. Who would have thought that Mister Silent Writer would be such an itch in the groin of the big chiefs, huh?"

It appears that this may be another warning. John *does* know interesting people indeed. That is how he has worked his way to very advantageous positions in contemporary society. He is wearing another permutation of an expensive leather jacket. His black silky shirt is accentuating his proud belly. The sleeve of the jacket is slightly pulled up to display a large golden wristwatch.

"At least you are a witness now. So if I vanish, maybe you'll notice." I wonder if I am joking as I say this.

"So Lee is gone, huh."

"Yeah, she cried."

"It's a practical move, though. You see how sons of bitches are jumping ship these days."

"Hmm" he is telling the truth.

"I heard of a pile of guys who flew to some obscure country in Eastern Europe perhaps, to seek asylum, only to be imprisoned, beaten like dogs and sent back. Only to be beaten like dogs and imprisoned again when they got back. This life," he sighs with raised eyebrows, "it is a bitch, no?"

"So it would seem, ferrah."

I take a swig of my beer, and John does the same. We are in the locksmith's living room, following a game of European league football. The furniture is cluttered but the television screen is large. The game is only beginning. The locksmith has gone to the kitchen to see to the refrigeration of the beers. His children have been exiled to their friends' homes for the night and his wife is probably keeping another abandoned wife company. There are four of us in the room. The other two men live further down the road. They are arguing about who is going to win the match. I look up at the wall above the television screen and see a faded picture of the locksmith and his wife in a park. He has his foot lifted on a rock. He is wearing grey bell-bottoms and has a disco shirt on to compliment his large shades and Afro hairdo. The man in the picture miraculously lacks the obstinate paunch that defines the locksmith today. His wife is about twenty kilos lighter and twenty years younger. She is wearing a semi-braided Afro and a risqué miniskirt that looks brown. And her tight top reveals the reason the locksmith fell in love with her. I laugh out loud. John looks up and I point at the picture.

"Not that again," he says, "Every time we come here you have to go and harass my brother about that picture."

The locksmith walks in.

"Hey, sasha those were the days." He is looking at the image.

"Who the fuck is the guy with your wife in the picture?" I tease loudly much to the amusement of the men.

"It's your father," he retorts and takes a seat.

"Those were the days indeed," I say, "So what did you say about my house, man? You'll find someone, yeah?"

"No problem, champion," says the locksmith, "how much should they pay for rent."

I look to John, not bothered to figure out these matters myself.

"I'll let you know after I look around to see what the market is like," John says to the locksmith.

"You have to be the landlord as well, make sure the tenants don't burn it down. And you can have a cut to pay for this satellite TV. How's that?" I propose.

"Sounds good, man," he slurs, "just don't forget to visit."

"As long as there's beer and soccer," I say.

With that, the matter of my old house is taken care of. The game is slow, so we pass the time by giving our professional critiques of the players. Soon we are comparing the teams we are watching to our own football teams. There is a range of feelings about this.

"Those fuckers don't even know how to kick a ball," yells the locksmith.

"It's the administration, the coaches are terrible," says a sympathizer, "if we had coaches like these teams, we would have worked our way to the top already."

"True, look at Senegal and Nigeria. They get to the World Cup,"

"We did better in the old days with the post-colonial coaches," says John adding fuel to the debate.

"Those fucking Boers and their dogs," says the locksmith inappropriately.

By half-time the conversation has smoothly morphed into thoughts on political and social administration.

"John said you may be in trouble, Champion. Is that true?" asks one of the men.

"I have been warned," I say simply.

"Those fucking dogs," says the locksmith. It's unclear what he is talking about.

"You write, no? I have never read your things, books are too expensive and besides my mind is not a great tool of thought."

"I don't write much, it's nothing…"

"Bloody crap man," interjects the locksmith, "you say it like it is." He rises and leaves the room.

We all hear him causing havoc in the back room. He returns with a book and throws it at the one who lacks the great tool of thought. I am quite stunned that my own neighbor has read something I have written. The book is passed around. John flips through a few pages. And in the great spirit of Zimbabwean ethic, the locksmith gives the book away.

"I have read it, pass it on."

"Maybe my daughter will read it," says the man, "she is the one I break my back for to send her to school."

"Give it to me when you're done," says the other man.

"You should play it safe, *shasha*." The locksmith is looking at me.

At that we rise go outside to smoke and others go to relieve themselves. The sun is setting slowly. The orange glow, the harbinger of night, spreads its cloth over the neighborhood naturally. There is a pothole in the road right before us and it seems the locksmith has been trying to fill it with cigarette butts. Standing by the roadside, inhaling the cigarette, I smile.

The locksmith, he has read my stuff. Never judge a book by its cover. He probably knows a little more of my mind than anyone else. I laugh out loud and John looks at me.

"The child has gone mad," he says to the locksmith.

"Haven't we all," he responds loudly, startling the passerby walking on the road.

"This life," I sigh, "it is a bitch, no?" I pass John's saying to the locksmith.

With that my cigarette is done. I wait for the others to finish. We get back inside just in time for the second half of the match to begin. The crowd cheers. And we are absorbed once more in the game. I look up at the picture of the young locksmith again and grin. I wonder what stories he has left in the dust that have been blown away.

After the match, we all pile into John's car and head to the open bar. Night has just signed in and there are a few cars on the road. I am seated next to John and the three others are in the back with the locksmith, drunk as a hyena, sitting in the middle. John had chosen to use the tin-can Toyota again. The Bar-and-*Braai* is located on the outskirts of the wound of civility, the high-density suburbs. It is a bar under the sky, where they sell alcohol and meat and *sadza* along with a few vegetables. On arriving we find that the party has already begun. Cars are parked in a failed simulation of order and grill stands are planted haphazardly in front of the bar building. Men are standing outside around grills enjoying raucous conversation and even louder music. We are lucky to find a free grill on the edges of the crowd. For a fixed sum we can get as much firewood as we need for the rest of the night. John, our gracious sponsor for the evening, pulls out a brick of money and throws it at the quieter man. We all agree that the meat is of utmost importance. In a culture where being vegetarian means you require a smaller piece of meat, vegetables are usually abandoned, quite literally, for the pleasures of the flesh.

"This is true living," says one man.

"Even in times of hunger and suffering, the black man will make time for a party," laughs the locksmith.

All around us are grown men with large bellies living out a weekend ritual. Most are men who have staggered here from the other side of the poverty line to indulge in the conviviality. They are a sort of tourist. Once the morning is nigh, they will leave as they came and the blur of class difference that was created will solidify once more. In the meantime the joys of social class may cross-breed indiscriminately. There are as many as twenty to thirty grills, each with at least five people around it. More people will come, and grills will be shared. So will alcohol and food. Friends will be made and our laughter shall be a mockery of the times. I am placing wood in the grill and getting to work lighting it. John gets newspaper from the other grill to light it. The grill is made of a rusty old metal barrel cut in half with holes punched through the bottom. The wire frame on top is also rusty and made of cheap recycled wire. The contraption is mounted on to a masterfully welded four-legged frame of metal piping. The beginnings of the fire are smoky as I blow the breath of life into it. The smell of the smoke is a lovely memory. I can almost taste the wood through the smell.

"Keep going, Champion," John teases.

"Do you know," sputters the locksmith, "in other countries they use gas for the *braai*? Or charcoal that is ready made." Then he shakes his head as though in pity, "They have no idea how to enjoy their meat."

I ignore the locksmith, as I am focused on the task at hand.

"Very true, mahn!" says a voice.

I turn to see who has hijacked the conversation. And standing next to John is a tallish bloke with thin and well kept locks. He is holding a Lion beer in his hand, the sacrilege. Who on earth drinks that stuff?

"Mine if we join you?" he says congenially, "Dem outta grill 'ere."

He has an accent of sorts. We see that he is with another guy. This one's shorter. And dressed in a blue shirt and grey trousers. He is also drinking a Lion. What is wrong with these folks? I almost feel the urge to save their souls.

"No sweat," says John, "Name's John," he shakes hands with the man.

The neighbor returns with a dish full of meat and some spices wrapped in plastic pouches. He puts it down. The fire is up and running.

"Name's Desmond," he says confidently, "Dis ma brother-in-law to be." He points at the guy he's with.

The guy looks a bit uncomfortable, and cautious. He sips his beer oddly. I can tell he is not a seasoned drinker. He is too kind to his beer. Too polite. He is holding it near the bottom with his right hand and his left is holding the top of the bottle. Desmond clarifies the issue, as he is clearly the more outgoing.

"I'm from Jamaica, I marry 'is sister so I come here to do official traditional wedding." So that's the accent.

"Jamaica!" says the locksmith, "I could have sworn you and I grew up together, haha."

"True say, people say I look like I'm Zimbabwean."

"That explains why you're drinking Lion." I say and the brother-in-law flinches slightly as though confessing to his crime.

"We'll show you real beer, my friend," says John, "Let's get another round." John reaches into his pockets but the Jamaican stops him.

"'Son me, no problem." He pays for the round and John advises him to pick either Castle or Zambezi.

After the refreshments arrive and the fire is ready for the meat, the conversations begin. The two neighbors are still contemplating the disappointment of the soccer match which ended in a heart-breaking tie of one goal each.

"Jamaica is good in soccer, no?" asks one of them.

"We're better at cricket," responds Desmond coolly.

"We used to be good too."

"So do you like what you've seen so far?" John asks, I can tell he is trying to sniff out a political topic.

"Same as Jamaica, just a little worse." His face is lit by the glow and obscured by the smoke. His features squint in the mild smoke, "My girl said this is the real Zimbabwe, so she made my bro'n'law bring me 'ere."

"The real Zimbabwe is everywhere," mutters the locksmith who has been poking at the meat on the grill.

"What's up in Jamaica?" asks John as he fights the digression, "What do you do there?"

So with the curved-tongue accent of strained truth he begins. We learn that he is a banker. He goes on to outline how his island has been robbed by the West and how intricacies of international banking and the sacrilegious cross-conditionality of the debt ensnare them. All this is told in the rhythmic drift of Patois. He outlines the nature of gang wars, corruption and so forth. John conjures up parallels in Zimbabwean society. Apparently, Desmond went to university in America and met his fiancé there. His descriptions of his home form themselves into a barbwire lullaby that mothers sing to their infants preparing them for the thorny path of life. We stand there drinking our beers paying attention to the man till he is done.

"Black skin…our damnation," my tongue slips.

"It has nothing to do with race or ethnicity, man. That's everyone's cop-out excuse."

"Just what my grandfather used to say."

"'S part true," says Desmond.

They continue on that strand of thought and I stare at the fire intently. The chunks of meat are being grilled. They are juicy and thick, they taunt me with their sumptuousness and I see the locksmith getting excited as he stabs at it with the prong.

"Get ready, gentlemen," says the locksmith almost drooling.

"Pass me the knife," I say.

Soon we are all biting into the blasphemously delicious meat while I place the second round on the grill. My taste buds, now sated, fall asleep and I return to my thoughts. I stare past the meat into the fire. The suggestive dance of the flames. They appear and disappear at their will like the promises of a false lover. Only the coals are consistent in their fluid glow. Sparks are spat out gently and the heat bakes my face very, very slowly. I almost feel myself shrink and dive in to the flame for cleansing. The invitations of the flame are silenced by the music, which is getting louder. I look up and around the fire. John is engaged in conversation with the Jamaican. The neighbors have adopted the brother-in-law and they are still rambling on about the soccer game. The locksmith has vanished, probably to relieve himself. Around us is a forest of western clothing and cacao colored faces turned orange by fires. Smoke rises and laughter blows through the forest and a river of music washes through us all.

* * *

Baobabs in Heaven

There is no magic where I come from. No laughter. I do not come across bubbles of happy energy while roaming in the woods. No. There is no magic. Only fading hopes scribbled on the toilet paper of yesterday. I do not find magical mentors of spiritual apexes nor friends to hold my hand. I let go and fall forever. My beauty is not coupled with supernatural acuteness and sensual awareness. My thoughts are damp and moist like dirty, old cloth in dark corners of the basement.

We are escorting the unnecessarily expensive coffin to its last stop. The slow-motion, weeping swarm follows the coffin. Dust is raised in the arid scape as the weepers traverse the few hundred feet to the other end of Serio's compound where others of his family are buried. The ground is naked and dry like the voices of the people surrounding and supporting the coffin. The cool surfaces of tattered, tired drums are being beaten in the bored gaze of the morning light. I am glad we are almost done here. I follow at a distance.

We awoke at the crack of dawn from a wakeful sleep colored by the pigments of grief. Scalding thick tea was served with large slices of thick dry bread. I burnt my tongue on the metal cup but was glad to be receiving the tea. It reminded me of how much I missed tea. I had made a mental note to drink more tea when I got back to the city. Later there were speeches given by the family and friends. They were tearful and bland lies told to give an image of what a brilliant person the faithful departed was. But I sat and listened. It appears Serio's brother had been the peacekeeper in the family, the cool-headed one. The buffer. The most memorable speech was by the youngest brother of the family. He sorrowfully described how this dead man was not just another tale of a hunter who had gone out and returned home with nothing on his back. That this was in fact the only person in the family worth a gasp. The man had broken down and cried as he talked of how close he was to his brother. To peoples' surprise and shame, he began to yell about hypocrites among the mourners who came to sate their own grieves and also the hunger for gossip about the cause of the death. We all knew what he was talking about. He was then dragged from our knowing guilt by those who felt he had said enough. People had shaken their heads and sighed saying that grief does this to people. I knew he had cast light on the darker recesses of the gathering's thoughts. The unspoken truth of the disease that had claimed the dead man remained a shadow lurking beneath our feet. One that only becomes evident when we stoop so low as to gossip, or when the sun of our conscience is setting and the shadow grows taller.

Now the ground beneath our feet on the way to the grave carries our many stout shadows. The soil is in large, hard clumps apart from a path made for single-file human traffic. To walk we have to raise our knees quite high to avoid stubbing a toe or falling over. Half way to the grave we stop for a moment of silence and respect. A sweaty reverend drops an inaudible feeble prayer. I think to myself that if that prayer was a reference letter to get to Heaven, then Serio's brother had better get ready for warmer climates. People's heads are bowed and there is the occasional "amen" sighed as positive reinforcement for the weak prayer. My mind takes a stride in its own direction: Heaven is within you and all around you. These were the words from the gospel of Timothy, the one that the folks in the Vatican would pummel you with a chalice for reading. I look around myself to see if this is true. The heaven all around me – the Village - is sad. Their faith is parched and hope is blurred from decades of listening to the same senile preacher and sleeping with the same whore in tedious alternation. The heaven within me is a story of my childhood, far away and colorful. There is no magic here, or maybe it is just now, or times like now when the world is as bland as the bread I was fed for breakfast.

* * *

Tonight *Ambuya* is tired. She had spent the whole day asleep. Her body is not well, but her storytelling is as strong as a baobab tree. She sighs and coughs a little. Tonight there are only three of us seated around the fire: grandfather, myself and her. This is unusual. A neighbor had passed away two days ago and was buried yesterday. So the other children are not here as they were probably not allowed to come over. My cousins are asleep. But I stayed with grandmother. Grandfather is also here because the neighbor was a good friend – his *sahwira*. I do not know how he died. But *Sekuru* is drinking beer out of a gourd and smoking.

"The story shall continue," says grandmother in a low tone, "life does not wait, our hearts beat till they are tired." She glances at my grandfather who is looking into the fire quietly.

He is far away. Smoke from the cigarette is swirling about his face and he is silent. The hood of smoke makes him look tired and old. *Ambuya* pokes the embers with a stick and tosses a log into them. In a few seconds the sparks turn into flames and the three of us disappear into the past: *Ambuya* with her fatigue, *Sekuru* with his defeat and I with my imagination tree.

"The Basket Weaver walked behind the large man in silence for many days. They would stop twice a day to eat. They never spoke to each other. And their eyes did not meet. They had only looked at each other once when the Basket Weaver had freed the *Zindoga*. The loner's expressionless face had extended its understanding from behind dark eyes and he turned to the dark forest. Basket Weaver followed." She coughed a little and shifted her weight.

"The oracle had occasionally appeared before them in the forest. They followed her form silently. They were two men walking different journeys on the same path. Life is sometimes like that. Sometimes two different journeys can be on the same path."

I hear a sniffle and I turn to look at grandfather. He is rubbing his eyes with his thumb and forefinger. In his left hand the dejected cigarette glows from behind a long protrusion of ash. He looks like he is shivering.

"Yes, and sometimes different paths lead to the same place," I wonder if she has noticed, "but these men were taking the same path to different places. The Basket Weaver watched in awe as the giant pushed trees over to make bridges over rivers and as he hunted animals with his bare hands. And the *Zindoga* observed quietly as the Weaver made reed pouches to carry water and wove rope baskets to carry food. Night and day were the same in the forest, so they slept whenever they were tired. One day they came across great danger."

I can tell that even grandfather is listening. I lean forward tentatively.

"Before them it stood. Its large teeth the size of an axe blade and its eyes deep in its skull.

"Now what could they do? Two men on the same path to different places encounter Fear. Perhaps they would meet again. As soon as it had come, it was gone. The two turned and saw the Oracle further up the path. They continued to walk."

Grandfather rises with a sigh, I hear his knees crack.

"Tomorrow has come," he mumbles gently as he leaves.

"It is tomorrow, *Sekuru*," I watch him and wonder if he will sleep.

* * *

After the burial, the crowd sits to eat lunch before leaving. The bull that had been slaughtered is finally ready to feed the masses. As Jeremiah and I sit with the men eating meager shares of meat and morsels of *sadza*, heads turn at the sound of shouting. We all rise and see four men emerge from behind a hut arguing angrily. Three of them surround one and are yelling about disrespect of the dead. The fellow being chastised is lacking in remorse. He is large and proud. Something about his manner is very familiar. I see that he is talking about coming to pay his respects to the living as well. Serio goes to see what the problem is. As they speak, I catch Jeremiah glancing at me momentarily. It is sooner than we hoped. We go and flank Serio.

"We don't want any trouble," he is saying.

"Trouble started a long time ago, but we are just here to pay our respects like I said."

He is not alone. A group of at least twenty is with him. They are bearing no weapons but they are clearly looking for trouble. They are talking aloud and in vulgar tones, but not at anyone. I know they are just here to pick a fight. And that they have been sent. I feel a few people looking at Jeremiah and me.

More men from the funeral are moving closer to us, but they still seem a little confused.

"I think you should leave," Serio says feebly.

"But we have not seen the grave," says the leader in an obnoxious tone.

His crew stands behind him. This is a stand-off. Two groups of people facing each other. The group I am in is clearly less accustomed to this exhibit of neo-primitivism. Besides, we are still in the funeral mode.

"We must see the grave," says the leader of the group.

"To piss on it," mutters one of his cronies. Bad move.

"What?" This is Serio's little brother, the one who had given the passionate speech earlier.

He is already advancing towards the chap that had blasphemed. I can see that this situation could explode easily as everyone is now advancing. Voices are being raised by both sides. Jeremiah is still standing next to Serio. I jump forward and catch his little brother before he gets to the leader of the mercenaries. I almost laugh at how unfair a fight it would have been. Serio's brother is small and thin. His flesh has been eaten away by an excessive affinity for marijuana and alcohol. He is yelling obscenities interjected with the demand that I release him. So I am sandwiched between him and the large leader guy. I can smell alcohol on the breath of the flailing sibling. Other men step in and pull him away to the back of the crowd. I can see that at the back of the funeral crowd, axes and hoes had miraculously materialized and are raised high. I turn to the boss guy.

"This is a funeral, you may pay your respects some other time." I feel Jeremiah at my side. Serio is on the other side.

"And if we don't?" Another bad move.

In a flash, there is the unmistakable sound of a gruesomely loud clap. The large man is staggering back and Jeremiah is pulling back his open palm. I jump in between two large men this time and on either side of them men are pushing each other and pulling at each others' collars. The large man whistles sharply. The signal is understood. And people release each other. Some are still cussing and spitting. The two large men stare over my head at each other. The invader leader is heaving, and his face has the neat dent of Jeremiah's palm. It can see it throbbing. A little saliva is on the cheek opposite that of the assault. Jeremiah stares at him steadily, with the dark look that makes my adrenaline run.

"This is not over," he says to Jeremiah.

"Have a safe journey," I say.

"You city guys think you're funny," he turns and leaves.

His army follows, leaving behind a trail of threats and evil promises. I am pleased to find no smell of fear when I turn back to the men that behind us. Jeremiah is given many pats on the back. He does not respond. People now ask us to confirm the rumors. We simply say that they had disrespected us. The dead man is forgotten. Young men are hoping for a fight. Older men sniff their tobacco groaning about how the times have changed. And the chief, who had watched from a distance, remains quiet. The white stubble on his head and chin looks terribly frail on his skin. He leans on his cane as he sits. I watch him closely, to see what remains unsaid. I watch him dread the future.

* * *

Sugar, Spice and Pornographic Piety

Squinting at the morning sun, I sigh and sit up tossing my bed covers to one side. My head is throbbing. My tongue is dry and the sweet taste of beer has turned putrid on my tongue while I slept. The chilly air nibbles at my shoulders making me shudder. I get to the bathroom and pull out my toothbrush from the cabinet. The door creaks loudly and I wonder if it has ever done that before. After three minutes of hard scrubbing, I experience the glorious feeling that can only be brought about by a freshly cleaned mouth. The mirror plays a trick on me by changing my face into that of a stranger. The only things familiar are my eyes and weariness. They make me look observant and wise. Like a keeper of secrets. Too much is lost in the ocean of words we paddle around in. Language is what we use to forget. Even faces can be forgotten using language. Like when people disappear and they become euphemisms. They are relegated to the past tense.

I fill up the tub and get inside. The water rises slowly. It is warm and stings a little as it touches my sleep-dried skin. Lying down with knees raised I go under the water and hold my breath. Years of childhood practice and hydro-foolery have taught me how to keep the water from going into my nose. I hold my breath and count in my mind. One, two, three. Being under water is like flying. I imagine that this is what it is like to die unafraid and content. Twenty-nine, thirty, thirty-one. My lungs voice their discomfort and my head begins to get hot. Forty, forty-one, forty-two. I feel my throat pushing itself to open but I fight it. My mind moves to Lee as my lungs begin to burn. I feel my body beginning to hate me. Fifty-nine – SIXTY! I come up slowly and exhale fast. Through a deep inhale, I relive my time with Lee. And I let it go in a single long exhalation.

My publisher told me that he has had good luck in Europe and Scandinavia with the work. There may even be a few translations in line. He also told me not to hesitate to let him know if I decide to take his offer on changing countries.

Take me from my home, or worse yet: give me a new one.

In the kitchen, mukoma has made some breakfast. Scrambled eggs and tea, the bread is laid out too. And the table is set for one. After eating I sit on the veranda. There are things swimming through the dreams in my head. *Mukoma's* wife is back and recovering in their home. It was a strange thing that happened to her. I guess it is happening to a lot of people. Empathy stumbles clumsily to the front of my mind. Sometimes the world gets so large it fills up your heart to exploding point. You become so small that you disappear and take your true form of nothingness.

The roads are the usual tumult of air filled with diesel fumes and van drivers' curses. I am looking at the ground as I walk. I avoid bumping into people who are in more of a rush than myself. People with important things to do, like earning a living. Looking down I pass by many sorts of shoes. Old ones mostly that have endured the test of time through the grace of meticulous up-keep and polishing. Some shoes are drastically more pitiful than others. A particular pair of notice has one of the shoes flashing a glimpse of a black-socked toe out of its open mouth. While the other is in need of the laces that its opinionated other possessed. Some of the women are in stockings of odd colors. I am prejudiced against women's stockings and even more so against petticoats. This is probably due to the childhood trauma of mustached, hairy-legged (and everything else) aunts who thought we were too young to know or be repulsed by the inner workings of under garments. I pass a long, very long line, which I trace to an ATM many meters later. Shops will not take checks. This creates an interesting predicament.

"Hey there, mister," chimes a familiar voice.

Raising my eyes I see a little girl not more than six years old. She is carrying a bright purple satchel. The child is wearing a red hat — oversized and a green sweater. The itsy-bitsy shoes with reflectors make me smile. She is looking at me with well deserved, I guess, distrust. Her little eyebrows are frowning and her pouting lips let me know who is in charge. She stares unflinchingly and I smile. On raising my eyes further, I observe her guide. In stylish faded jeans and a sky-blue top, brown shades and black suede heels, I see Julia beaming at me. Her hair is newly permed, and it looks good.

"Julia."

"How goes?" she looks happy to see me. A little too happy.

"Who is this, mama?" squeals the little bundle of joy.

"Be polite, Tinashe."

"Who is he?" she is still staring at me with juvenile truculence.

"Is this yours?" I nod at the child.

"It's my husband's."

"That's great," I realize my tone may be off.

"Is it?"

"Really," I stutter, "I like the hair."

"Who is he?" Tinashe has raised her voice.

"My friend, honey. He's my friend." Julia soothes, and to me, "My ex-husband."

"I wanna go!"

What is wrong with this kid? Back in the day, my parents would have slapped me silly for such ill mannerisms. I could not so much as cough in public without a thorough spanking for the inappropriate reflex.

"It's ice-cream day," Julia explains.

Mother and child begin to walk off.

"Hey," I say. She turns around, "You have my number."

She smiles as she is tugged away by the girl. *Sugar and spice my arse*, I think to myself as I turn away. Little girls are despotic. I smile. But the kid is quite cute. I like children. They make me feel like there is hope…for anything.

Four hours later I arrive home. My dinner is prepared and while I eating, I receive a call from Julia. We talk for a while or rather she talks and I listen. She has a lot to tell. And in an hour, I have absorbed more information about her life than I have about my own. Her words are lively and excited. Her language is simple and direct.

"You don't speak very much," she observes.

"I like to listen."

"Yeah, but don't you ever have anything to say?"

"It's all been said before."

"I've known a lot of people who aren't big speakers," she insists, "but they've all come around."

"Should I be afraid?"

"Too much fear breeds misery in the land," she says, much to my surprise.

"Ngugi wa Thiong'o!" I name the author.

"*Matigari!*" the title.

"You've read that?" I don't hide my enthusiasm.

"In high school." She laughs.

"Beautiful work, black Jesus, an ebony Magdalene and a culture which in that light, appeared to have the pornographic piety of captive Africanisms…" I catch myself.

"You seem quite passionate about this subject," untamed glee emanating from the other end of the line.

"Can you blame me?"

"You almost sounded like a critic or writer or something."

"Well…" but before I can respond.

"Speaking of high school…" and off she goes again.

So I listen. Her voice turns into a soothing hum. And I occasionally make sounds that imply that I am paying attention. But I am really just feeding my soul with the sound of her voice. After a few more seconds I feel it is the right time to interject with a quick question on the subject in order to sustain this simulation of attentiveness. It pleases her that I do so. I have become good at multi-tasking in my mind so I also use the time to flip through book I got from the university library a little too long ago. Lee used to talk a lot too. Her phone calls were a good time for me to sit down and write checks for my bills or, back in university, to write a draft for an essay. It's not that I don't pay attention to what people say. I manage somehow to sufficiently do both, unless I really don't care about what the person is saying.

"You want to know a secret?" she says.

I stop flipping pages.

"Depends on the secret," disguising my curiosity.

"You're no fun."

"I'm all ears," I learnt that most questions women ask you are a trap, or maybe I am just very proficient at digging myself into deep mucky holes.

"Well I'm not telling you,"

"Well maybe next time…"

There is a long silence. Then a sigh from the other end of the line. I smile inwardly. She changes the topic and, in minutes she hits another tangent, then another.   All the while I listen and fill my mind with images of what she is saying and I do my best to listen to what she is not saying. This is what I am drawn to. The power behind her words. Her strength. The happiness and joy that is lurking behind each and every phrase. The stories in the shadows that she so tactfully avoids with her language and the delicious colors created by the sound of her tongue in her mouth and the breath passing between her teeth. Her happiness on the other end of the line is material and I imagine – in fact I know, the gestures she is making as she speaks. Like my grandmother taught me to, I learn much about her from what she does not say.

"Why don't you ask me any questions?" she asks.

"I figure you'll tell me when you are ready."

"You sound tired."

"Just very relaxed," I confess.

"Well, I'm going to bed, I have to work tomorrow,"

"Good night then."

"You're strange," she says as though giving a verdict.

"Aren't we all?"

"I'd like to see you tomorrow," she says carefully.

"Same time, same place."

"Liquor store?"

"Yup."

"Good night," she laughs.

"Bye."

And as I hang up the house becomes very large and empty. I brush my teeth and fall asleep almost immediately.

I am rudely awakened from a strangely familiar and unsettling dream by a loud knock on my door.   My heart jumps.

There must be a problem with the poor man's wife again. Yawning, I pull on my pants and shirt and almost fall over from sleepy dizziness as I walk to toward the door. The three locks are cold on my fingers. On opening the door I am blinded by a flashlight.

"You are the writer," I cannot tell if that is a question or not.

The torch is lowered and my eyes to come alive and I see three men. The one with the torch is big and wears overalls and Wellingtons.

"You must come with us." A man in a grey suit is standing holding something in his hand that looks like a rod of sorts.

"What is this about?" I say as if I don't know.

The third man is also wearing overalls. I cannot see faces clearly but I can tell they are not up for dallying around.

"Is there a problem, sir?" This is *mukoma* who must have been awakened by the sounds too.

He looks worried and, frankly, quite pathetic.

"Go back to sleep," says the second man in the overalls.

He seems well accustomed to being uncouth.

"Ok," I say and step outside and lock the door behind, "*Mukoma*," he is still standing there with frightful wide eyes, "you'll find a few phone numbers, in the house. Call John and let him know."

I can tell this momentarily shifts the power grip in the situation, but Grey Suit takes it back.

"Let's go, sir." I wonder how much longer he'll feign politeness.

Grey Suit walks in front and I follow him, with Overalls and Wellington flanking me. We get outside the gate and there is a *Santana* waiting. The driver of the vehicle is a shadow. Grey Suit sits in the passenger side and I am 'assisted' into the back of the truck, the place criminals, both innocent and guilty, occupy. There, in the cold company of Wellington and Overalls I feel the cold metal on my buttocks. I still have not seen any of their faces. But I suppose that is the purpose of carrying out this activity at such an hour. It occurs to me that I should be afraid.

As we are bouncing about in the back I can feel the two henchmen staring at me. I watch the streetlights pass me by on the outside. They seem very distant. And I know they are. The truck becomes a vacuum from which no sound, emotion or experiences can leave or be made known to the outside. I should be afraid. But I already did all the fearing I had to do when I experienced that false call the other night. Wellington, seated uncomfortably close to me, grabs my right arm and clips on a handcuff. Before he speaks I pass him my other hand. My lack of resistance must have confused him for he hesitates for an instant. Then he clicks the second wrist more tightly, almost cruelly. Overalls, seated across from me, leans over and puts a cloth over my head. I cannot see. My heart begins to race but I take a big sigh and it slows down slightly. The cloth over my head smells like many faces. It has a sinister softness. It feels like stories of fear on my skin. I am becoming part of a large story. I do not speak. I hear my heartbeat in my ears and my nose begins to run. My stomach gets uncomfortable. Maybe I should have asked Julia what her secret was. The hairs on my skin reach out to the world as though to compensate for my imposed blindness. They are searching for something familiar. But I am lost to the world. Is this what it is like to disappear? As I am sucked into the night by this loathed symbol of our suffocation. I suddenly find comfort in a little joke I once shared in such a vehicle with an officer of the law. I try to smile, but it hurts. It would be a lie.

* * *

Requiem of Our Longing

"One night, on the path, the two men sat by the fire in silence. They had finished their meal. Now they stared into the flames. Without words they had come to know each other. That's how it was in those days. Words are heavy and large, so if you wanted to know people you had to lose the words."

Our young minds struggled to understand this concept of no words. How could that be. *Ambuya* used words and spun tales so well. How could we ever know these tales without words? The fire crackled and spat its rebuke. And our minds were hushed again.

"Then there was a visitor. He just showed up out of no-where, with the moon in his eyes. Do you know who this was?" she looks at us.

We nod our heads knowingly.

"Yes, the Reed Flute Traveler." Her joyful cackle surprises us. "You see, you knew when no words had been said. He sat by the fire and the Weaver offered him food and he ate. Then he played music. With his flute, he painted all the things that had been spoken in the language of silence. They would hear it again from time to time in their journey, but they would never see him again...at least not with their eyes"

* * *

The mountain is just as I had remembered it only with a little less vegetation. The grass is thigh high and the shrubs waist high. Trees stand apart from each other connected only by the gust of wind that carries short messages and secrets. Jeremiah decided to stay at the compound after the funeral, "just in case". I wanted to go up the mountain. It is on the edge of the village. It used to stand tall and proud the way I had remembered it. Maybe that is because I was small. It used to be green and alive too. From a distance one used to be able to see the mountain guarding the village like a protective cousin: too distant to be intimate but clearly more powerful and capable. Now it stands like a disowned uncle, wretched and expended. But it still has the memories written in its terrain. And my body is moving over it like the fingers of a blind man reading Braille. I am finding memories in the combinations of landmarks and my mind is titillated. It gets steeper as I climb. I am breathing softly for fear of disturbing the sleeping mountain. I listen to my footsteps and each sound I am making to separate them from the sounds of the mountain. A sudden rustle stops me in mid-stride. My eyes quickly follow the sound. A small tree, with half its leaves gone, stands serenely. My gaze slides down the artfully textured bark and in the blanket of small, dry leaves at the base of the tree, I behold a dazzling sight. The caramel colored, dry leaves are pulsing ever so slightly. And the spread of leaves slowly transforms itself into a pattern of similarly colored diamonds. The pattern winds hypnotically towards a hard flat diamond-shaped head. It is a Gaboon viper lying quietly bathed in meditative solitude about a meter from my feet. I once met a man who had suffered the bite of one such snake. He had to lose his forearm. I smile. Such beauty is beyond magical. The snake does not move. Looking into its eyes I can see the pattern on its back is continued by its pupil. I catch myself salivating and move on.

I like snakes. I have always considered them to be misunderstood victims of the occult. I know a few superstitions concerning snakes. Some are thought to be harbingers of death. Like the Cape File snake, some believe that if you see it, someone in your family is going to die. And that if a Python crosses your path something terrible is going to happen. There are no snakes in the city except maybe the Brown house snake. I once suggested we keep one in the ceiling of our house to eat the rats. My mother chased me out of the room with a wooden spoon and had to be calmed down. She did not speak to me for days afterwards. I get to the top of the mountain smiling.

I look over the village and my smile disappears. A cold gust of wind hits my face. I stand on a rock that I used to stand on as a child. People look small on the dirt roads down below. The lake is drying out and the river is nothing but sand. A few children are playing in the soccer field outside the school and a bedraggled lorry is huffing and puffing down the road leaving a petty cloud of dust behind it. The land is thirsty. And I realize that I too am thirsty. It is drab and sad. As I stand there, the leaves that are green in my mind wither and fall at my feet. I let go of my dream. My past is left dangling like an incomplete sentence - parched. I put my palms behind my head and let the wind run over me, around me and through me. I laugh deep and loud, till a small tear squeezes its way out of my eye. I laugh. What else can I do?

On the way down the mountain I hop and skip over rocks quickly. I fall and sit down hard on a rock. Cursing, I dust my pants. As the pain is seeping out of me, I limp with a palm on my bum. The sound of moving water meets my ear and I ride my curiosity towards it. There is a little brook. This is strange to me. There is thick greenness all along the little stream. An energetic trickle skips along the stones and pebbles. I guess there is a little spring somewhere further up. A large rock invites me to sit down close to the water. And as I do so I learn a strange truth: brooks sing. I have read many a pathetic poet writing in sad romantic rhymes about singing brooks and I have often considered it stupid. But it is true. I laugh again and lean into the brook to bring my ears closer. As the water falls between a few rocks, it makes a tickling mid-tone pitch sound comprised of three or four notes that playfully and randomly dance about together. I silently apologize to all the poets' works I have desecrated wrongfully and lean back on the rock. Rays glitter through the foliage and fall on my face. And here in this secret place that has survived the decay of time, I kneel down in my mind and piece together a little souvenir for my memory.

Eventide presents itself quietly as I am walking back into the compound. I hunger and thirst immensely. I kick off my sandals by the doorstep of my room and head towards the light in the kitchen. As I enter the kitchen I find Jeremiah saying farewell to a visitor. I recognize the man's face from the night at the township.

"City boy," he says happily, "So you now roam the forests like a madman?"

"Just trying to remember," I shake his hand.

"The times have changed my brother, and so has the land. There is little that one can still recognize."

"That is true,"

"You have caught me on my way out, I must eat the food of my wives or else they will be jealous." He puts on his hat and walks out into the darkness.

Jeremiah pulls out his snuff bottle. Surrounded by the walls of the little hut, he looks like a great bull in the pasture. Shadows swim on his face and a young smoky fire crackles with childish effrontery. He sighs and taps the snuff bottle on the bench.

"You are in time for the food," he sighs.

And as if on cue, the second wife brings in a dish of water to wash our hands. Kneels before me with the dish and a jar full of water. I place my hands over the dish and she pours water onto them. I rub them together to watch the clean water become murky as it comes out from the under my hands into the dish. It is cold. I move my hands away and she stops pouring. She does not look at me but moves on to Jeremiah and does the same. It occurs to me that Jeremiah is one of the few people who have more than one wife, even in this village. It is a dying tradition – an expensive one in this day and age. Yet it is not strange. As she leaves, the senior wife enters with a pot of beer and places it at Jeremiah's feet, he grunts his gratitude. She serves us and she rises leaves.

"Tell one of the children to bring us more firewood," he tells her.

I am already reaching for my plate.

"Excuse me," I say as I begin to dig into the steaming meal.

The stew is thick, the vegetables are well cooked. And the meat is good. I smack my lips and lick my fingers as I go.

"This food is great, *shasha*," I mutter between mouthfuls.

"You're just hungry."

"You sound tired," I don't look up.

"Bloody funerals! A guy can't sleep."

"True, I didn't sleep either." I lick my fingers again, "Get your wives to be good to you tonight," I suggest slyly.

"That's the only sensible thing you've said since you got here!"

"What do you mean?" I pretend to be hurt.

"Getting me into fights,"

"You're the one who starts them! You could have gotten us killed today."

"They had no manners."

"They'll be back for us, you know."

"No sweat, *shasha*." He says, "Perhaps you should return to the city." He sounds concerned.

"You just want to hoard all the action!"

With that our fatalistic pact is sealed. I wash my hands after a second helping. We move on to the beer. The second wife comes in and takes away the used cutlery in silence. Outside a frog croaks in the darkness hoping to find a companion or at least a momentary pelvic affiliate. My grandmother once told me that if there were no frogs, there would be no water. So I take comfort in knowing that there is water somewhere, like in that secret place I came across. Somewhere in all this despair and futility, a bubbling brook of energy, light and hope is singing softly in the green shade of peace and longing.

"Why did you come back, *sahwira*?" his tongue is untied.

He has called me *sahwira*. Man's closest friend with whom all is shared: from thoughts to possessions. Under the suffocating blanket of hardship, a man can expect none other than this friend to be there. When a man dies it is the duty of this friend to see to it that the proceedings go well and that the family of the departed is taken care of. If I have no food in my house, I can enter Jeremiah's house and carry out a large piece of meat and not be questioned because I am his *sahwira*. It means we are friends between whom unsaid things can be understood. He has never called me this before. I take a large gulp of the mature brew and wipe my lips with the back of my hand. I stare at the fire until my eyes begin to water. The smoke makes me wince and reminds me that I am fragile. That I am human. I rub my eyes.

"So that we can walk on the same path to different places. Is that not what friends do... *sahwira?*"

The sound of scurrying footsteps approaches and Jari's little son enters holding a child-sized stack of fire wood. He places the wood by his father's feet and sniffles. Jeremiah rubs the little fellow's head lovingly.

"What took you so long, mister?" he says smiling.

"I had to chop some first."

The child has a husky little brave voice.

"Good man, take a sip." Jeremiah gives the boy the gourd.

The boy smiles a little shyly but accepts the gourd. It is clearly not a first time for him. His little head is almost the same size as the gourd. He looks like he going to fall over under its weight while tipping his head back. I laugh. When he gives back the gourd, he is licking off the sizable beer mustache he has grown. Jeremiah wipes off a little drip from the kid's chin with his large thumb.

"Now go to bed," he shoves the youngster gently to the door, "and don't tell your mother," he says to the child's back.

The kid scampers off happily with his head ducked. His little bare feet create a lightened pitter-patter canticle that momentarily enlivens the night. I hear him release a tiny cough, then the sound is gone. Jeremiah tosses a log into the fire and sparks fly frantically about. Flames begin to rise. They are larger and more ominous. I do not like the way they are moving. I notice that the frog can no longer be heard. The glow is portentous. Jeremiah is silent. The world is silent.

Simultaneously, we lift our faces and look at each other. Faintly, in the very far off distance we can hear a lorry engine coming in our direction. I rise and go outside. The sand is cold on the ground. The night air is dry and chilled. Jeremiah follows holding the gourd. He passes it to me and I take a sip.

Looking up I see the quarter moon low in the sky. The stars are reclaiming their quota of brightness in the aftermath of the full moon's reign. Jeremiah turns to the flickering, orange rectangle of light from the kitchen and walks in. He reemerges with a machete and the handle of a hoe and stands next to me. The sound of the lorry is getting louder and we can see hints of headlights bobbing in and out of view in the distance. I take the machete. Jeremiah walks calmly to the room of his first wife, walks in and comes out with the son who had brought us the firewood. I can tell from the silhouettes that the chap is drowsy and rubbing his eyes. Jeremiah's large shadow leans over and mumbles something to the little shape. In an instant the little fellow is scurrying out of the compound headed to the neighbor's compound. The headlights are now visible and approaching. Jeremiah's senior wife comes out.

"Father of the house, is something wrong?"

"Return inside and lock the doors." Jeremiah is brief.

She obeys, and so does the second wife who was on her way out. Jeremiah whistles and his mangy dogs sprint to his side barking wildly.

"This way," and he walks away.

I follow him behind his hut and wait there with him. I realize I still have the gourd. I take a sip. Jeremiah takes the final swig and tosses the gourd away. I stand behind his broad shoulders. We can see the road from our positions. The lorry's yellow lights are bright and we hear the engine slowing down as it nears us. It turns shakily into the compound and we slam ourselves flat against the back of the hut to dodge the lights. The two dogs scurry to the lorry and bark madly as it is coming to a halt in the center of the compound. The lorry is full of people. They are quietly leaping out as the lorry is stopping. We hear a few thuds and the dogs are whining and howling pitifully. There are whispers from the stooped shadows. Walking stealthily around the edge of the huts, we see some people enter the kitchen followed by angry urgent whispers. There is a scream from one of huts as they start banging at the doors. Jeremiah picks up a brick with his free hand, and I follow suit.

"Hit the lights!" he whispers.

Surprising me, he charges out from behind the hut knocking a man down. I follow behind him and still holding my brick. Jeremiah throws his brick at the vehicle and the head light explodes in a spray of sparks and sound.

"There they are!" a voice yells.

In the light of the one-eyed lorry I see Jeremiah take down two guys with quick swings of the club. I get to the lorry and swing the brick into the remaining light source. A spark burns my skin. Still holding the brick I turn and smash in the face of an aggressor who falls over and I blindly swing my machete down on him. With this, amateur guerilla warfare commences in the belly of night. Submerged in a blur of shadows and shouts Jeremiah and I participate in our own requiem. I know we cannot win. But, goddamnit, we will burn a memory into these fuckers' minds before we go. I have lost my hearing again. My palm is sweaty and slippery on the machete blade. Jeremiah is grunting. For a moment, I long for the peaceful song of the mountain brook. But life is only long enough for a joke, and eternity, for a laugh. The door of the kitchen hut, an orange rectangle, becomes the light at the end of our tunnel.

* * *

City of Oracles

Twelve ways to die, most of them involve a pair of scissors. In the little time I am given to recover or rather, to regain consciousness, I find myself designing my own funeral. Who will be there and what will they say, think, dream or do? I have always wondered what happened at the funerals of those who disappear. Do people wait a while to decide whether or not the person is dead? Do they decide for a moment, a sad little moment of fury, that they will rise up and fight for the country they lost, the child they lost in time? Wind will blow against the grief-taut skin of black-clad mothers. Men will sit red-eyed containing their remorse like a familiar regret of a foolish youth. Wasps will buzz about a compound irate due to this incomprehensible intrusion. And I, dead I, will lie in the cool shade of a mango tree, in the cool comfort of a box, dressed in a suit that I had probably neglected for a lifetime – this is of course assuming that I am ever found. May be they would bury an empty coffin, or better yet, bury me in the sky.

My eyes strain in the dimness to see. There is nothing. The ground is hard, cold metal and the damp chill around me smells rotten. My face is on the floor and I am naked. A sharp pain is working its way up my back. I cannot even remember where I was beaten. Just a damp, dull pain working its way up my back. My throat is dry and I am thirsty. The side of my face on the ground begins to tingle and my ear is ringing. I can smell the blood at the back of my throat. My wrists are cuffed behind my back and I am breathing restrainedly but heavily as I would after a long bout of lovemaking. Fatigue mingles with the blood in my veins and becomes the overtone of my pulse. My eyes are swollen shut but I force them open to see the approaching gumboots. I hear their cold scraping against the floor. These boots walk differently from the other ones that have been in and out of the creaking metal door. These boots are more purposive, less brisk, a little more efficient in their stride. I can tell from the lightness of the scrape to the heel of the sole and the hushed tap of the toes when they touch the ground. I can also tell by the gentle malice of the bottom of the boot on the upturned side of my face. After coughing up a blob of coagulating blood, my body allows itself to pass out.

* * *

Pain reminds us again and again that we are soft. Sometimes we forget. I remember as a child forgetting my human-ness many times only to be reminded by the rough sting, thud or pop of pain I stupidly inflicted on myself. There are times though when we are well aware of our softness, the tenderness of our skin and the fresh moisture of our bones, the tears behind our eyelids and the fluids our body contains. These are the times we are afraid. Afraid of dying, of getting hurt, fearing imminent pain.

When I was found I did not speak, I just shivered and cried like a child. An indefinable infinitude of darkness crouched in hiding. Through the swollenness my face had become hard-set and cool. My mind alive, but with all the wrong things. I did not speak. The doctors said I was absolutely fine. I lay in the hospital. My tongue was thick and heavy. I had many visitors come through to see me but it was like everybody had changed. My publisher came and made a scene, called in his journalist friends, took pictures of me and conjured a statement from his arse to compensate for my silence. He said he'd get me the fuck out; I only needed to say the word. He probably felt that these events would eke the sales of my books internationally. I did not speak. He also said that turmoil and suffering is the stuff that writing material is made of. As he sprinkled this sermon through his tobacco stained teeth I felt something unpleasant rise within me. He must have seen it for he left awkwardly and abruptly. John stopped by with a cigar in his lips. He shook his head and tried to make me talk. He told me he would get to the bottom of this and find out who did this and see to it that I am compensated. There was something unusually familiar about his tone. Like the politicians in rural areas making promises. Julia came too, she touched me and cried. I did not speak. It's not that I did not want to, there was just nothing to say. I was tired. I was angry. I was afraid. I was very tired. *Mukoma* brought me food every other day. His eyes were afraid, he shook his head, coughed and rubbed his stubby chin over and over again. He respected my silence.

The light in the hospital room was bright. There was the sound of traffic during the day and sound of suffering and dying echoed in the hallways at night. The nights were difficult. A nurse came in to change my bandaging and check my pulse and blood pressure regularly. She was awkward and afraid not of me but of what I represented. Her face was painfully pleasant. I think she was glad that I did not speak. Julia came everyday to spend a while with me. She would bring a book and read to herself while sitting beside me, sometimes she would touch me. I do not know how she found out where I was. She did not speak either. Sometimes tears fought their way out of me and I would shake. Sometimes my pulse was higher than it should have been. The doctors said my blood pressure was a little high too. They made me go to see the hospital psychiatrist. He looked tired and underpaid. He also looked uncomfortable in his white hospital coat. The furrow of his narrow brow told me that he was uncomfortable. He seemed unaccustomed to dealing with sane patients. He was as frank as the times permit. He said that perhaps I am being quiet because that is what they want me to do. Then he shuffled uncomfortably, cleared his throat and began to flip through files. I told him to fix his tie.

The locksmith stopped by the hospital; he was drunk. He made me smile. But then he began to speak – shout rather - about things that everyone already knew, like who had done this to me, and why and the "fucking dogs." Needless to say he was escorted out arms flailing and round belly hanging out of his World Cup t-shirt. The days were loud the nights were louder. In the day, the noise came from outside – outside the hospital, out side my room. In the night the noise came from inside. My beard was growing out again, my hair is unkempt and tangled. My nails got a little long. And I could feel wax accumulating in my ears. I lay in bed not because I couldn't walk but because I didn't want to, just like I didn't want to speak. Julia brought me a newspaper once. I did not read it. She told me that the administration had cancelled some zeros from our currency. That they were working out some deal to share power with the opposition. I raised an eyebrow. She said it was really unhealthy that I chose not to speak. They sent me back to the psychiatrist before I left. He was wearing a bright yellow tie with Persian patterns on it and a venomous green shirt under the time-stained white coat. After asking if I wanted to talk about it, he cleared his throat and shuffled uncomfortably. I felt something unpleasant rise within me once again, and I think he saw it for he wished me well and sent me off awkwardly.

I was offered a wheelchair to leave the hospital in, but I declined. I limped out raggedly absorbing the stares from the hospital staff. *Mukoma* had brought my car keys and left them after driving in with Julia. She had left my car in the lot. I wore the clothes she had put together for me. Walking out of the hospital, the hairs on my skin reached out to the world and the scorching sunshine passionately welcomed me. I went to my car and cringed with the creaking of the door. I sat in my car for a while and listened to the aching of my body. I picked up the pack of cigarettes and threw it out the open door. Pulling out of the hospital I was greeted by the blaring, obnoxious aural intrusions of the public transport terminus that is right outside the gate. The vendors were still risking their lives by breaking the law. A beggar was rummaging through the trash undisturbed. People were walking to and fro busily in their work clothes.

* * *

Grandmother once told me about a City of Oracles where nothing really happened and no one ever spoke. It was a land of silence not because the people – the oracles - were mute, but because they all knew what would be said, what would happen and when. It was a secret place. As secret as the land of tears. Ambuya said, as Jeremiah and I stared at her, that the Oracles were not sad, nor were they sullen, though they did not smile. They were all woman, daughters, taken by the Water Spirit – chosen. But because their families had wept for them, they could not return to their villages. Occasionally, a new young girl would walk from the bank of the river to live in this City

of Oracles. They were uninterested in strangers, as they were
when the Basket Weaver and the *Zindoga* came upon this magical silent plateau with large rising stone walls. There were not
guards at the entrance, but about the land there were women
- all silent. They looked up from their work in the fields as
the two men passed. They were weeding the crop or plowing,
gardening and herding. There were all the makings of a village, but no men and large structures of stone held together with no mortar. And the women just glanced at the men
as they passed. A blank stare like that of a grazing elephant
that knows it is too large to be moved by a hare. That is what
Grandmother said and in my mind I pictured women of all sorts
large, small, thin, fat, old, young, beautiful or ugly like some
of my aunts. All shapes and sizes of daughters, silent and burdened by their infinitude of knowledge. I thought of how sad
they may be.

"Isn't it hard to be quiet?" I asked my grandmother.

"Women are used to it."

I think I saw a subtle but heavy frown fall on her brow and
disappear in the flicker of the flame. Jeremiah, next to me, was
staring deep into the fire walking through the City of Oracles
in his own imagination.

"They know what will happen to the two men, don't they."
His voice was sad. It was also a little husky from the day before
when we bathed in cold water because we were too lazy to heat
the water. *Ambuya* looked up at little Jeremiah with such tenderness as I had never seen before in the expression of her grey
eyes. She looked at him for a long time, while he still stared
into the fire. A moth flew into the hut with unnatural grace.
It was as large as a little bird. It fluttered about Jeremiah and
created ominous shadows on the roof of the hut. Then it dove
into the fire suddenly, and vanished in burst of hissing flame

and brought us out of stillness. Jeremiah was still staring into the fire unaffected, and *Ambuya* was still watching him.

The story continued: the men were fed in silence by these women who knew everything. They knew not to speak for the Weaver had heard of this city in his learning from strange conversations of his weaving days. He had been told that a breaking of the silence in this city could make you disappear forever. But that is not why he was silent, there was just nothing to say. He also knew that it was a city that one could only pass through once in their life, not because people didn't want to pass through it again but because the city was never in the same place. You could not find the city, the city would find you. The men left the city, or perhaps it left them for when they awoke they were back on the path.

Ambuya looked once more at Jeremiah with watery eyes. Then she said it was time to go to sleep. Jeremiah and I walked out into the night. I followed quietly behind him and watched the silent shadow of his walk. The cool, kind breeze of the night seemed to remind me of things I had forgotten that I know. Things that had not happened yet. My imagination created a city of oracles about me in the darkness. Shapes of women became alive and watched the two of us walk by. They were silent. I was not afraid. I turned to look at the hut that we left and saw *Ambuya* standing in the orange rectangle of the doorway watching us. Her little bundled figure leaning on the large stick she had begun to use as a cane. She too became an Oracle in my mind. I wondered what she knew.

* * *

John is steering the four-wheel drive *Mitsubishi Pajero*. The CD player is dishing out a sample of up-beat South African house music. John said he had something to show me. We are on the road we usually took to get to the farm where we buy meat. The car is very new; in fact it is reeking of new-ness. I begin to get an idea of what John is going to show me. I turn off the air conditioning and roll down the window. The sweet smell of elephant grass and wet soil fill the vehicle. The sky is cloudy with another forlorn promise of long awaited rain. If only the land would be quenched and showers of blessings would finally fall upon our upturned faces. There may be a little drizzle. Or then again the clouds may just be passing through on their way to give water to the eastern highlands of the country. The land where they grow the coffee, tea, apples and strawberries. The green, high mountains where I have never been so close to the sky.

There are no cattle in the fields, no young herders in overalls in the pastures on either side of the highway. We catch up to a rickety lorry that drowns us in its generous outlet of fumes of diesel smelling smoke as it crawls leisurely along the tarmac. In the open rear are six men laughing animatedly and talking loudly. They are also passing round a container of the Chibuku brew. They turn to us and wave energetically, one of them raises the brew up high. I give them the thumbs-up sign out the window and they laugh and clap. The lorry slides over to the outer side of the road and signals John to pass. He does so slowly. And the men cheer as we pass and John pumps the steering wheel to let out two short jovial blasts from the horn. This makes the men cheer even more. I wave as we pass and the lorry driver lets out his own rusty beeps from his pitiful horn.

In minutes we are traversing that familiar road to that cattle farm. This time it is much more comfortable because of the vehicle. The tires lift a cloud of dust behind us and a few resting birds are rudely awakened. I watch them go. They are butter storks, and they slowly come into formation as they retreat. The expansive desire inside me is constricted by my ribs. I want to fly. I have always wanted to fly. As a child I would pray to God for a pair of wings like the seraphim or cherubim or anything at all. But what does blonde-haired, blue-eyed Jesus know about the infinitude of my Africanness. About the way I sometimes bleed from the inside from pain that is not mine. But I prayed for wings...I never got them.

"Ok Champion," John is pulling into the clearing by the kraal, "we're here."

I still haven't spoken much since I left the hospital. And I don't really care to do so. Looking about, there are cattle in the pen and some of the workers are walking towards us with large grins on their faces. The old chap with the springy step is lagging behind. John lets his belly protrude out of his shirt and he sways on his toes a little as he pushed his hand deep into his pocket. As always his shiny, thick, golden wristwatch is visible because his left jacket sleeve is always coincidentally pull up just a notch.

"Good morning, sir," chimes the first to arrive.

"Today we shall celebrate," John says, "just us men, huh?"

The other men show up and offer their greeting and nod their heads. I look up and see that the clouds in the sky are clearing up. Once again, it was a false promise of rain.

"A beer for each man," John commands, "you know what we like. Put it on my account." He coughs and pulls out a handkerchief to wipe imaginary sweat as though all that talking has expended his energy.

"Yes, boss." And the fellow is off.

"Don't forget the meat," John reminds him.

I contemplate this new wiping gesture of John's and also that I don't recall him carrying a handkerchief before. I also contemplate the fact that he is "boss".

"When did you get it?" I say quietly.

" He he he," and he waits for what he feels to be an appropriate pause for royalty as the other men take this to be their cue to leave their boss to prepare the feast.

"Not too long ago, Champion," he finally answers the question.

He tries to read my expression. I give him nothing.

"The workers were skeptical at first, you know. Afraid even. But I made it clear that they needn't worry unnecessarily. We are all grown men you see, huh?" He flicks hand as though to laugh at the pettiness of the workers worries. "In the end they are getting more out of it. So here we are. This beautiful piece of land, a real diamond, huh?" I remain silent. "I know what some people think, Champion, that I sold out, that it is unethical. But I assure you if I had not taken it, some other frog would have leapt onto this throne."

Realizing he is getting nowhere, John pulls out a cigar and lights it. After the first inhalation he spits on the ground then sighs. He glances at me then changes his tone as he rubs his head.

"Anyway, the actual surprise is your piece..." and he adds quickly, almost testily, "that is, if you want it of course. One hundred and seventy three acres. Yeah it's pretty small, but good for intensive animal husbandry and horticulture. There's a nice water source and," he says proudly, "it's right next to me."

I am surprised.

"Think a about it for a few minutes," he doesn't wait for my answer and walks off to join the men at the grill.

I follow silently thinking about the rain that passed us by. And the jovial group of working men whose lives are for sale from one landowner to the next. Pawns . The beer is good on my tongue and fizzles down my throat. The meat smells good but my lower lip still hurts a little as I put the bottle to it.

"You look as though you have faced an ordeal, sir," says the older man looking at me, "what happened?"

"Blessing of the large fist," I say.

"My brother is a victim of a misunderstanding," John says trying to make light of if.

"They feed you with the left and beat you with the right," the old man shakes his head, "I have never come across a spring that gives sweet water one day and bitter water the next."

"But today we drink sweet water," John pushes in and raises his bottle.

The men laugh nervously in accordance with the will of the man who raised their pay. A dark cloud settles over my mood to replace the ones that had passed overhead. But I do not speak. I have not written since I left the hospital. My laptop had been 'stolen'. Mukoma had apologized and I told him I understand. My publisher promptly gifted me another laptop on credit. But still I cannot write. I sit at the screen and rage bubbles to the front of my mind. Droplets of anger form on my fingertips and I begin to shake. I have tried to write but I cannot. The 'celebration' dies down as the lazy sun goes to nest in the west. I get in the car with John and leave. He turns down the music and speaks without looking at me. He is scratching his chest with his left hand. The huge shiny watch jingling as he does so. The handkerchief emerges from his pocket and he wipes his forehead.

"About the land," he says.

"I'll take it."

"Good, because there are those who think you should."

I am quiet.

"And in good faith, I'll give you twenty percent of my piece. You won't have to do much work, but you are more of a people person. You are good with words." The political voice again.

"Ok."

"That's a smart thing to do, Champion. The times call for no martyrs and saints. Just practical people."

I absorb his words reluctantly and cautiously. His words are like a mattock: two tools with one handle. There is a truth and a lie. I roll down the electric window with the push of a button and close my eyes to feel the air on my face. John turns up the music, it is Vusi Mahlasela: *how did you respond/ to the language of guns, knives, knuckles and boots/ how did you respond/ oh Troubadour?* His voice on the stereo makes my eyes moist, but I smile. Life is a long time. John clears his throat and changes the disc and it's back to the loud bass of the *kwaito*. I rest my mind by conjuring up the few happy memories and thoughts that remain in my mind – memories of contentment.

* * *

A Quiet Obsession

The truth of the matter is that life ends in a dream. Nothing hurts nothing laughs, except dryly. Nothing hurts, not even the punches and kicks that rain on our bodies as we lie roped up in the back of the lorry. The dream continues as our blood is made death black in the light of the dying moon. I am on my back, my unfeeling cold back is also a part of the dream. I am looking up at the stars that shine down on my beaten face. My view is obstructed by the occasional boot or fist. Turning in this dream, I see the face of Jeremiah, facing me. He is on his stomach and his eyes look sleepy – in the bad way. A black slime, like the slime that is my own blood, is trickling out the corner of his lips into a puddle on the floor to mingle with my own blood puddle. The blood of my friend and that from myself comes together in a will-crushing pool of broken tenderness. But Jeremiah is smiling, through his sleepy eyes. I gasp to speak but gurgle blood instead...and Jeremiah blinks. There is only the hum of the lorry engine, the cold clear night to escort us and a smooth dream framed by the moonlit silhouettes of the executants of our misfortune.

We are in a dream; we must be for I am crying. Graceful, painless dream tears move down the side of my head to join the puddle of blood. Jeremiah is not crying. He is larger than life before me, larger than tears. In this dream, we cannot feel the pain, hate and fear that they want us to feel. We are beyond it. I think to myself that Jeremiah never wrote me a letter in response to the ones I sent him. I think to myself that he knows me more than I know him. He is strange to me. I watch him with oracle eyes gifted to me by the tragic presage of this night. The air on my skin feels warm, but I know this is part of the dream. That in fact we are very, very cold, that we are half-way to heaven. Jeremiah expands before my eyes and becomes very large, his eyes staring at me but past me. There is an echo of words from the frame of our dream that I do not understand that bounces up against the bubble of this reverie. A large object swings down heavily onto the side of Jeremiah's face. His expression widens and I see moth wings burst into flames in the center of his eyes. A tear much too small for his body rolls out of his left eye, down into his right eye and into our puddle of dreams. The flame in his eyes dies. His tears look like blood and his blood looks like oil.

The edge of my dream begins to mumble and mutter urgently. Voices are raised and bodies shaken. My eyes are on Jeremiah's ashen irises robbed of their fire. I worship the illusion of his absent vitality. A silhouette reaches down to stab at the large man. I burst out in a dream scream – one that I cannot hear, but feel in the depth of my being. I am grabbed and tossed out of the moving lorry on to the gravel road. Landing on my shoulder, I feel the pain of dreamtime. Still rolling, I get up with my arms bound and run after the lorry. The moon paints the lorry into a grey ghost-bus. I am left in a cloud of cemetery-blue dust. My legs cannot carry me fast enough. I reach out to Jeremiah desperately. I cannot see him. From my lungs, a deafening muteness rushes forth. A memory flashes before me: Jeremiah chasing me while I am in a bus. I trip, fall and land on my face. Tasting blood in my mouth, I feel myself pulled out the dream by a blast of cold air that is the night. They have taken him. My feet are slow and heavy, hurting, dragging. As I chase the lorry – chase Jeremiah. Jeremiah.

* * *

They found him before they found me. They found Jeremiah. Large and dead. In the woods far from the village. In the mountains. They found him thorn-bitten, beaten and dead. His large arms rigid and cold, his calloused palms rock solid. His eyes open and ashen. They found him dead, my brother - my friend. They found me small, shivering and cold after two days on a road less traveled. They found me incomprehensible, like the muttering laughter of a hyena in the night. They say I babbled endlessly till I saw Jeremiah. Dead. I melted and clawed his body like a lost soul trying to return to its host. They say I beat the men that tried to stop me from digging through the skin of his corpse. They had to knock me out. They also say I cried and called Jeremiah's name through the night. I shook and convulsed and my voice changed. They say I called Jeremiah's wives to me and bade them farewell, that I called his oldest son and told him to be good and not to miss me. They say I convulsed and fell unconscious. They called the village priest and he just shook his head and prayed. I do not know if this is true, I was not there.

* * *

I walk out of the hut and the sun seeps into my aching bones. I am in Jeremiah's compound. The shaking in my legs reminds me that I am a battered man. That absence of Jeremiah and his cigarettes reminds me that I am a living man. I am an angry man. The compound is silent. It is many days after Jeremiah's burial. There have been men visiting me and women visiting his wives. They have taken care of me. Jeremiah's second wife is walking out of the kitchen and she sees me. She is taken aback by the fact that I am on my feet, though I lean on the doorframe for support. She scurries towards me.

"Did you rest well?"

"Yes" I lie.

"We are still preparing the afternoon meal"

"It is well."

I stagger forward and she gasps and catches me before I fall. I am weaker than I thought and heavier than she thought for she stumbles under my weight.

"Over there," I point to the spot Jeremiah and I sat in the mornings.

She helps me to the little mango tree. Her breathing is heavy by the time we get there. There is a little wooden stool and I drop myself on to it a little less than gracefully. I put my hand on the ground to catch myself from falling. The sand is cool on my palm despite the sun.

"I will get a mat," she says.

She stands looking at me for a while. My gaze moves from her feet upwards but she turns and leaves hurriedly before it reaches her eyes. Sitting down, I try to think but I cannot. I call one of the children and tell him to go to Jeremiah's room and get the tobacco and snuff. The fellow looks at me for a while – oddly. Then he turns and goes to his father's room and emerges with the goods.

"Hey!" it is the senior wife, "What are you doing in there?" She is not pleased.

The little boy stops in mid-stride.

"I asked him to get tobacco." I say in a hoarse voice and cough unhealthily; I can taste blood in my throat.

I am Jeremiah's *sahwira* so I can use the tobacco regardless of what others may feel. She knows this. I know this. It's not that I am taking liberties, I just feel tobacco is the least of liberties she needs to be concerned about - not that I intend to take any others. I am certain that to an extent she is glad I am still around. Since there may have already been a line of well-wishers and 'friends' lining up to inherit, forcibly, what Jeremiah may have left behind.

"Oh, I did not see you," she says with a cold apologetic voice, "is your body well?" her tone is tense.

"As well as can be." I don't think she likes me.

I don't blame her. As the boy gives me the snuff, rolling paper and tobacco, he says:

"They killed my father." And waits for what seems an eternity looking at me as if for an answer.

I tap snuff in to my left palm and take a pinch with my right. Sweat is beginning to rise on my neck and the lad is still standing before me.

"Yes... they did," I sigh avoiding his eyes.

I take the pinch to my nose and take it in loudly. A shiver runs down my back. And my head shakes. I let out an ugly sneeze. It has been years since I have had snuff. I rub my nose frantically. The boy is still standing there.

"They did not kill you," he says.

Looking at the child in the face, I can see his anger. Perhaps it is at me.

"No, they did not," and I take a pinch of snuff to my other nostril.

My head becomes lighter. The boy turns on his heels and runs away, past the kitchen into the fields. His mother, the senior wife yells after him, but he keeps running. She shoots me a glance and walks into the kitchen. I sit outside and breathe deeply as I roll a cigarette. I try to think again but I cannot. My body feels light. The sun feels good on my skin, the air tastes fresh. Everything seems to be speaking to me in a language I don't understand. I try to listen but I cannot think. The warmth of the sun seems to be singing to me, and the breeze whispering in my ear. The very taste of the cigarette and the smoke before my eyes as I burn the cigarette; they all seem to be trying to tell me something. Or perhaps my desperation is leading me to look for meaning in all the wrong places. Looking out at the entrance of the compound, I see people passing by on the road. A little dog goes by followed by a cart pulled by skeletal cattle. A bug passes by my ear and I swat at it only to discover a new pain in my body. I try to think but I cannot. My thoughts are broken by the sound of the second wife approaching. She places before me a bowl of steaming sadza and cultured milk. I can smell the smoky steam of the mealie meal and the sweetness of fermented milk. I am absorbed in the appearance of the food.

"What will you do?" Her voice sounds like my conscience.

"I'm going to kill them." The words almost surprise me too.

The phrase comes naturally. I try to think about what I just said but I cannot think. It is almost like someone else decided for me. I reach for the food. I don't know if she heard me, but she rises and leaves. I watch her feet leaving marks in the sand and raising a little dust. I try to think of what I just said but all I can think is how much sense it makes. Yes, I will settle a score. A life for a life. If the police are not willing to look into this, they have no reason to look into the death of another. Just one life, then I will leave this village. This place that was my home, this place that was Jeremiah's casket. This place that I love and hate. Then I will leave. This quiet obsession ferments and matures in my mind as I chew the food.

After eating the food, I wash my hands and lie down on the mat. I fall asleep almost immediately and a dream of heaven comes to me: a land of baobabs and blue silk; Jeremiah without a shadow; long grass of savannah gold. There is a black sun and the sand is silver. Jeremiah disappears before my eyes and in his place I see a large baobab tree coming towards me, or I am going towards it. I see a singing brook of blood flowing out of its trunk. Strips of silk are the leaves of the tree. There is no breeze so they hang - as still as silk. I wake up calm and clear: just one, then I will leave.

* * *

Ecclesiastes and the Bandana Boys

Heaven is trite. Hackneyed, like a story told over and over again, like political promises or the predictability of servitude. We go to take a sip of stale heaven every Sunday in church and leave with nothing but bad breath and a song to sing. A song tired of being sung. It's almost as though history is being rotisseried over the fire of stupidity till there is nothing but charred expectations on the dry bones of our experience. Sadness too is trite. After a while you cannot feel it and may actually prefer it. Like the analogy of the man who after being in a dungeon for a long time was released and he cried, Take me back to the dungeon it is too bright out here! I like the word trite because it seems to sum up my opinion of many things. It's kind of like Ecclesiastes put it: there is nothing new under the sun. But I know I am not separate from what I despise. Hope is trite. I am tired. It is my first walk since I left the hospital. In truth, it is against my better judgment to be out here in the city center on the day there is going to be a rally for the opposition party. God knows how they got the permit to do it. I thought I would pass by and eavesdrop. Already, as I approach the area of the rally, I see an increase in the number of roaming police. I am still a block away from the park where it is to take place.

The police are lounging in their vehicles having conversations. I wonder what the police talk about. It is inconceivable that they can have normal, senseless conversations like ordinary folk. In my mind there is a very solid wall between civilians and the law enforcer. My mind cannot even imagine what happens on the other side. Maybe they talk about sex. Or sports. Perhaps, the beating they intend to give, or about the stock market. My mind gives up, and moves back to civilian thoughts. My body is burning under the thin green shirt I am wearing even I undid three buttons and rolled up the sleeves.. I can feel my feet sweating in the shoes I am wearing. They have been sueded by age. I glance around to see if any of the police are watching and I quickly take a swig of my *Chateau* brandy and shove it back into my rear pocket. My head is light and my mood is dark. I spot two officers walking with Alsatians sniffing at every passer by. Their tongues are hanging out and they are panting. They are coming in my direction. I feel a tickle in my ear so I put my finger in it and wiggle it. The officers give me a glance not void of meaning as they pass by.

Approaching the open park, there is a welcoming committee of Santanas and fully geared riot police, dogs and municipal police in their navy blue pants and shiny black old boots, gray shirts and red eyes. The rally has already begun. There are a good two hundred people in the audience spread on the lawns before a cheap wooden stage upon which a young man is talking (and sweating) passionately. He wears a white t-shirt with a face printed on it. There are a few others with the white t-shirt on their back. The crowd is mostly young men and women. I find my way to a decent spot for listening and sit down surrounded by a few guys with rags tied about their heads as makeshift bandanas. They give me a pat on the back and welcome me like a long lost friend. In fact their enthusiasm is quite dangerous. They seem to be waiting for something.

"Welcome, shasha," they whisper loudly.

I wonder if it is wise to sit in this section of the gathering. At that moment the speaker on the stage bursts into song and the gathering gladly joins in. One or two people around me stand up and begin to dance thus raising the energy of the group. As the song is going on I am tapped on the back. I turn to see what they want and I am passed a rag made of old t-shirt cloth and a five liter bottle of water. I wet the rag generously and pass the bottle back. I receive another pat on the back. Now I am well equipped with the "varsity survival kit" as people fondly call this gift. I put the wet cloth into my pocket and decide to return the favor. I pull out my brandy take a deep gulp and pass it to the chap that gave me the rag. He grins and takes a swig and passes the bottle on. It disappears. Then more people stand up and join in the bastardized version of a liberation struggle hymn. A speaker gets on to the stage. I guess he's the one they have been waiting for because the crowd bursts into loud applause and the song becomes loud and raucous. People get onto their feet and stomp about. I am lifted to my feet and dragged closer to the front of the crowd, by my bandana buddies. With arms slung over my shoulders I am shaken and pulled to the rhythm. My aching body complains, but the contagious energy raises my spirits as I am assimilated into this mob. The speaker on stage raises his arms. I realize that we had made it to the front of the audience. The crowd's noise retreats into a series of whistles and applause.

The speaker is young with a youthful pubic beard sprouting randomly on his face. He is largish and his hair is very short. He wears the white t-shirt but I can see that under it, he has a shirt collar and a tie.

"What are we here for?" he begins his speech.

The crowd grows silent. He repeats the question in *Shona*. A random whistle jumps from the assembly. Followed by a tell us. He repeats the question in *Ndebele*. This draws applause from the waiting crowd followed by a series of ululations and whistles. The other two fellows on the stage raise their arms to hush the crowd so the man may proceed.

"I will tell you why we are here." Then a pause, "why we are not at home," another pause, "why we are not at work," more approbation and whistling then a pause, "Why we are not in *school*," and the crowd goes wild with frenzied support.

"I will tell you in the words of a man who knows truth, a man who knows freedom. The freedom we all long for. The true freedom that our forefathers fought for. Not the Mickey Mouse morsels of freedom that are illusions and briberies we accept at a greater cost." More whistles and a few people stand up to demonstrate their consent.

I turn my head to the back of the crowd and see that the police are in formation and attentive, not to the speech but to the people's movements.

"I will tell you in the words of a man, whose vision is un-clouded by the fear that is bred today. A man who longs for freedom and peace in the way we should all long for it. A man who loves his country. Our country."

By this point the crowd is a mix of applause, cheering and whistles. They are begging the speaker to tell them. To feed them this truth that he has found. Some are asking who this man he speaks of is. Tell us my brother! screams a female voice. The speaker raises his hands, and the solemnity of his face is almost heart breaking. It makes my heart ache, long for this truth he has. I too want to hear, to know why I am here and not at home. I too long to know who this man he speaks of is. Looking at the man on the stage, I see that his eyes are moist, mine too are moist. The crowd becomes silent. He pulls out a little piece of paper from his pocket and opens it up slowly.

He takes a deep breath and begins to read without looking at the paper.

My heart stops with the rise of his voice. The power of his tone. His voice shivers as he stretches out the words. At each comma he pauses. He lifts our hearts with his voice, shakes our fears loose and frees our very souls. My eyes open wide and I inhale as my heart jumps up and kicks my collarbone. The hairs on the back of my neck rise slowly and a tear glides down one of my cheeks. My spine becomes warm and weak. Recognition forms itself into a monster in my mind as I realize gradually that the words he speaks are mine. They are words I wrote, but to hear them from this man is to hear them anew and afresh. He is not looking at the piece of paper, he is reciting them from his heart, his hand gestures and his voice rises as he approaches the end. The last few words are lost to the applause of the crowd which rises to its feet in a single large movement. The speaker is sweating and yelling, that is why we are here! That is why! I too am on my feet, but I do not applaud I stand in awe at what my words have done, what his words have done. I don't know if there was more to his speech, we will never know for already everyone has broken into song. The song that usually marks the end of all rallies – in violence. My mind spins into confusion as the crowd gains rhythm and momentum.

Toyi toyi
Hai!
Toyi toyi!
Hai
Hoo Left Right!
Hai

Everyone is in front of the stage and hopping from the left foot to the right in sync. Sticks have been raised in the air and cloths are being waved high. The speaker is still on the stage bathing in the glory of the moment when we see a police officer backed by five others and two dogs, walk up onto the stage. The crowd launches an avalanche of curses at the authorities. The song continues louder and darker.

Form the units!

Hai

And Fiiiight!

Hai

Form the units!

Hai

And Fiiiight!

The police begin to advance from behind us and encompass us in a cow-horn formation. My mind goes back to history class in high school: Tshaka Zulu, great warrior, dictator, and destroyer, founder of the cow-horn formation. I only hope our fate will not be like that of Tshaka's enemies. I can see the dogs by the stage getting restless too, they are barking and salivating. The police officer on stage is talking to the speaker in the din. He turns and raises his hands to the crowd, which then hushes itself apart from the isolated clear curses cast by hidden instigators. The speaker begins again as the crowd is sitting itself down. I sit and watch, relieved that the violence has been averted, at least temporarily.

"They say we are loud." he cries in a comical voice.

The crowd laughs and throws a variety of vulgarities at the police.

"Don't worry;" shouts the speaker as though to the officer, but clearly for all of us to hear, "they are cursing at the dogs."

Everyone laughs at the double meaning. The officer does not look amused and I think to myself that that was not a very diplomatic move by the speaker. The policeman is tapping a baton in his left hand. The speaker turns back to the crowd.

"They say we are too loud, we should be quiet." His tone changes, "we should be quiet about oppression, we should be quiet." A mumble of disagreement rises from the gathering. "We should be quiet about beatings. My brothers, we should be quiet about suffering. Let us not make noise. We must not awaken our leaders from their sleep in mansions while our stomachs grumble. We must not make noise. We must be quiet about corruption, inflation, starvation, abuse of human rights."

The crowd is yelling *No*. He goes on, with a vein throbbing in his forehead.

"We must be quiet. We must be quiet when we see our mothers scrounging in dumpsters to feed us, when our father's dignities are dragged through the gutters. Let us not make noise my sisters, when AIDS has claimed half the population, when we have no electricity, or water in our homes."

The crowd is applauding and a line of riot police officers has formed around the audience. They have the big fiberglass shields and helmets. They are a few feet beside me and the bandana boys. The speaker on stage does not relent.

"The officer's master would like us to be quiet. But wait my brothers." He raises his arms, " I ask you," he turns to the officers with the vicious canines and the officer on the stage, " Do *you* have electricity in your home, is your family going to bed on a full stomach..?" the crowd cheers and the song resumes itself.

The speaker does not finish as the officer strikes him once in the head powerfully. The speaker staggers and falls backwards. The crowd is hushed immediately. The fellows on stage in the white t-shirts are standing dumbstruck staring at their motionless mate. I jump onto the stage and kneel over the fallen body. The officer that had hit the man is standing over us, a little uncertain of his action. The crowd behind me has gotten to its feet and the bandana boys are scrambling onto the stage too. Tilting the speaker, I see that he is very unconscious and is bleeding from his ear. Then I put my ear to his chest and hear that his heart is still fighting the good fight.   A fat girl with a white t-shirt is on the stage and yelling and perspiring at the officer and attacking him with her claws. More students get onto the stage and the officer, in a moment of stupidity grabs the young obese lady thus increasing the chaos. Lost in the forest of shouts, legs and feet on the stage, I see that the speaker's fall had spilt the contents of his pockets, a wallet, a penknife and the piece of paper with the excerpt of my early novel. My ears get warm and a shiver rushes down my back as I reach for the penknife. My mind goes blind and I open my eyes as I am pulling the blade out of the officer's neck. A little spurt of blood frees itself from the man's body along with his soul.

There seems to be an eternity in which the whole gathering gasps and blinks unanimously. It is very quiet as a breeze walks by gently to observe this event. My lungs are empty and serene, my body feels light.   The officer is still falling slowly, with his hand on his neck, blood coming though his fingers and the disbelief of his mortality scribbled raggedly on his face. My fingers let go of the knife and it too falls forever. My eyes blink slowly to move me to the next frame of my life.

* * *

Trench Coat Mindslur

In a burst of winged virulence and a flurry of flight, the Bird appeared before the two men on the path, the Weaver fell backwards in surprise and let out a moan of agony as he twisted his ankle. Yes a minor detail in a tale: the twisting of an ankle. But it will be important for now you know that he will limp through the rest of the tale, crippled. The *Zindoga* dashed off right after the bird only to give a momentary glance over his shoulder as a farewell.

"Goodbyes are not always as pretty as we hope," Grandmother takes a tangent, "in the Liberation Struggle we said many goodbyes. Most of them rushed and some of them unsaid. People would leave in the blink of an eye, in the stutter of a tongue, and they would be gone. By the hand of a freedom fighter, and we would wonder what, or whose freedom they fought for, or by the hand of a colonizer and we would bend our faces in the pain of incomprehension. What did they fight for?" I knew grandmother had lost a child or two in the liberation struggle. I knew that one of my uncles had broken his own hand to avoid being drafted into the Rhodesian army; another had jumped out of a moving lorry to achieve the same goal. These are truths I had learnt in the beer smelling breathing of another funeral night when *Ambuya's* memories are agitated. Tonight the memories are flooded with her emotion as she sweeps us- Jeremiah and me - into a tale of action. For some reason it has only been Jeremiah and I attending these nighttime story sessions. I suppose the others think they are too grown up to hear them. But we are determined to hear this story to the end.

"Jumping over logs and through brush, skin tearing at the hacking of twigs and branches, the large man chased the Bird. Heaving heavy breathing that echoed all the way back to the fallen Weaver, the *Zindoga* chased the Bird, his mass breaking through walls of brush through promises of death and ensnarement in things he did not know. He ran till he caught up with her. His dreadlocks trailing behind his head, veined arms reaching hungrily into his loss. And in that moment the Bird burst into flame in his sight. It was gone. He came crashing down on the forest floor clasping nothing in his hands. It was then he realized that he would never find his bird. Because it was not his. It was then that he died, even though is took his body many weeks to realize this. In this time he roamed the forest till he came to its edge. There he sat and waited. He waited, he thought, for his bird, but instead it was for Death, in the form of soft music, in the form of a dream." *Ambuya's* voice was as loud as we have ever heard.

"He had never been a child, he could not recall it. And now he would take his true form as the guardian that stood in the glade between this world and the next. There at the edge of the forest he let go of his life. Not with a tear, but with a sigh. If you go to the edge of the forest today and stand in all silence and earnestness, you may hear the music. But do not try to find where it is coming from because it is coming from inside you. Your time has not come yet but when it does you'll see him; large before your eyes, silent his eyes dark like the Water Spirit's. He will let you pass into the forest if it is your time.

If it is not, then he will not. Do not fight him," she is looking at me, "he is your friend." The story is over and we rise to go to bed.

The next day we herd the cattle to the glade. To think that the glade between now and never is by our own village. We stand as the cattle graze and hear nothing. We sleep under a tree for an hour under the lazy sun. We hear nothing. Not the sound of a dying man from a folktale, not the burst of flames of the bird as it disappear. All we hear is a quiet breeze as we lie in the sun, the shuffle of cattle in the grass and each other's breathing.

* * *

The next day lands coldly on my chest with a heavy cloud, promising tumultuous rain. In the afternoon I see flocks of birds flying for cover, the cattle are restless in the kraal, and the dogs are quiet. The smell of thick fertile soil rubs itself against my nose. The wind picks up and throws around loose mats and leaves. The dust is happy to be moved by it. I stand by the door of the hut. Jeremiah's wives and children are in the kitchen. I smoke cigarettes and try to think of how I will do what I will do. The city has become a memory in the foggiest corners of my mind. It is almost unreal. I have forgotten it. But I know that when I return, this too will become a hazy shaded reminiscence - a mindslur. I finish off the smoke and turn around leaning on the doorframe watching the darkness creep over the earth. The wind stops almost suddenly having brought the clouds to their final stop. Heavy, angry raindrops land like fists on the dust. They fall individually, giving warning for those who have not made it to safe refuge yet. I turn around and go back into the hut scratching my chin, thinking that I should shave. My beard has grown out to a decent size.

My room is dark and smells like sweat and goat fur. The weather has made it this dark so that even the little window in the wall does not give me enough light. Sitting down on the stool I lean over to study my options. There is a club, the one Jeremiah carved. And there is the machete he won in our first encounter with the militia. And there is a plain knife I took from the kitchen. It is smallish and a little rusty at the handle. It as the haggard look of a malnourished hermit. The rain outside has picked up to full force. It roars for a few minutes before the flaws in my shelter confess their existence. The dripping from the roof turns into a steady trickle. I stand and take the bucket in the corner that I use to wash my face in the mornings. As I put it under the leak I hear someone at the door. The second wife is standing in the doorway a little wet. With her knees together she squats.

"The afternoon meal is ready," she has to raise her voice over the rain, "shall I bring it to you?"

"Yes, thank you."

She does not meet my eyes as she turns and runs into the rain. I return to my seat and pick up the knife. The silent thunder of my conscience is also promising rain: a downpour of dreams of blood splashing in the mud beneath hope-swollen feet.

* * *

I leave in the late afternoon. The rain has not yet let up. I am wearing a coat, a cheap sun hat and sandals and my feet are wet. My breathing is arduous as I am still not recovered. My left leg is painful, I limp on it slightly. The rain has become a drizzle and my thoughts are mangled in things that have nothing to do with the task ahead. Jeremiah's second wife had told me of the place they – the thugs – hung out. This was after I had expended much energy making love to her in the secret of the night. She had come and knocked on my door timidly while the rain was singing pitter-patter hymns in the darkness. I had buried myself deep within her mystery and clung to her convulsing in morbid ecstasy. She had cried afterwards with her back to me. Then she had told me where they would be. I did not ask how she knew, but I left in the afternoon headed for the township. All I have in my pockets is the rusty pitiful knife and enough money to get me back to the city. I left the rest of my money where the senior wife would find it. I left quietly so no one would know that I am gone. But my thoughts are no-where near my present ambition. The trench coat I am wearing is Jeremiah's; it keeps my body dry, but my feet and the bottom of my trousers are wet. The coat smells like leather, because that is what it is. I suddenly remember that this coat actually belonged to Jeremiah's great-uncle. The one that had fought in the Second World War and lived to tell the tale. He was al-ways ranting about how he fought side by side with the white man in the deserts of god-knows-where. He had two medals that he showed us every chance he could. He was drunk most of the time though. But it was many years before it became clear to me that he was another tragic case of diasporic refuse – exported, expended and returned. He even had a rifle with a bayonet at the end. It was rusted almost beyond recognition but it was evidence enough for us. It is this man's trench coat I am wearing. It has survived the ages and has been passed down. I know it belonged to some white man before, because the African soldiers of the World War never got new uniforms.

But as I walk towards the township, the place where she said they would be, my thinking strays farther from the task at hand. I wonder why we have been reduced to this instinctive killing. This hereditary culture of violence. It seems the xeno-phobia of our inherent past has squeezed its way into our being and has been passed on to our children. To myself. What the fuck is wrong with me - with us? So it came to pass that any problem we have, we are trained to beat it out: out of each other, out of the system. We are a violent people, a psychotic people – African. The trauma of primitivism and colonialism and many other schisms and –isms still run thick in our blood. My footsteps become heavy. The rusty knife in my pocket – the treacherous, pathetic angel of death - also becomes heavy. I am tired; my life is tired of what I have become. Of what they have made me. I am not afraid, just tired of how worn, how trite this path is. I am walking the same path to many differ-ent places. The rain courses down the coat and drips onto the dirt road that is eroding away quicker than we can fill it. I am suddenly, sadly reminded of my culture; browslack and dying. It is also eroding faster than I can take. It is as if everything is eroding, washing away into the roadside gutters. One of my teachers as a child, was a haggard looking man, deep creases in his face marking all the trails of his past and his dread of the future. He is the one that taught me the phrase "going to the dogs." I did not know what it meant. But he made it clear that everything had gone to the dogs before he got a hold of himself and stopped his old tobacco-breath heaving.

But I keep walking. A lot slower. Why do we do it? Africa – God bless us – has been hacking away at is own limbs for centuries now. Really, like in the Rwanda genocide: just at the utter of a word, they fucking hack each other to bits. Maybe it is because everybody wants to be a part of something bigger than themselves and death is most obviously bigger than eve-ryone. So we partake in this ritual of mortality, stupidly and blindly unaware that we are tools for other people's means. Is this our damnation: to sit in a distraught crater of self-pity and abnegation, hack ourselves to oblivion till we are so hopeless that all we can do is bleed on each other? Like the men that killed Jeremiah: What did they get out of it? The knife gets heavier in my pocket. And the rain gets wetter and colder, its lightness mocking me.

I arrive after four hours of walking; the sun is going down, not that it ever came out. The grayness is turning to black. The township is a strip of six or seven dilapidated little shops that are mostly closed. The bus stop is at the end of the strip. The old bus is parked there waiting for the last run to the city, which is at some ungodly hour of the morning. I walk to the bar. An age-stained dim light bulb is glowing dejectedly on the veranda of the bar and music is playing thinly ignored in the background. There are men sitting on empty crates on the veranda. Realizing that my victim-to-be is not here yet, I walk round to the back. There is a row of four soggy pit latrines leaning dangerously behind the bar in the rain. I spot an empty container of the Chibuku brew under a water tap on the back wall of the bar, my perfect disguise. I am as sober as a stone, but I begin to play my role. Picking up the empty container, I place it under one arm, pull the cheap hat over my face and traverse the darkening night back to the front of the bar. I sit on the floor at the corner of the veranda and lean against the wall. I am hoping that everyone will think I'm some silly bugger drunk out of his mind and leave me alone. Lazy zouk music is playing from some lonely corner out of fuzzy speakers.

The few men on the veranda do not even notice me apart from a little glance. After a few minutes I hear them talk about me for a little second.

"Look at that poor bloke," slurs one, "the night is still young and he is already visiting the ancestors." They all laugh.

I keep the hat over my face and do not move, I even fake a drunken snort to amuse them even more. Waiting on the cold floor I drift off into fitful sleep. My dream takes me to a subway where I am surrounded by panicking people waiting for a train. I am still wearing the World War coat. A train arrives in the gray dream and the door opens, looking over my shoulder I see medieval warfare in full form. People killing each other with spears, axes and swords. Everyone is running away from the war and getting on the train. Body parts, all gray, are flying about in the battle. That is when I catch a glimpse of Lee, bug-eyed and afraid. She is getting on the train too and staring at me. I see myself in the trench coat smile at Lee, turn around and walk into the iron-age battle calmly. The train leaves without me. I awaken with a start as someone is kicking my leg.

"Buy some booze or fuck off, old man," the bar owner is saying. I dig into my pocket and pull out enough money for a container of Chibuku.

The man snorts, grabs the money and returns with a full container. Keeping my face hidden I take the container and shake it a little before I open it. On popping the top, I am overwhelmed by the scent of fermentation. The brew is thick and sour on my tongue but I take it happily as it is the first drink I have had since — since Jeremiah. It is strange to be marking time using the memory of a friend. But then again, I have been doing that my whole life. When enough people die, they can become markers in time. Like my grandfather, who always recalled events in relation to other events, I can never use dates and times. But in a traumatized culture you can mark events based on loss and trauma. Things are never lost neatly though, like a messy abortion when the loss of the child is coupled with the decompositions of the laminaria inside the mother to cause a disease. Each loss in our culture leaves is mark. The soft

French lyrics from the stereo are flowing gently over my ears along with the intention of healing a lost love. That is when I see him. The big man who had interrupted the funeral with the mob of disrespectful dossers. Rage inflames itself within me and I feel my nostrils flare. Thinking of Jeremiah, tears form inside my eyes. I lift the brew to my face to take a sip to calm myself and also to conceal my face. The man has just arrived and is shaking people's hands merrily. They make room for him and he pulls up a crate and seats himself. I can tell he is half drunk already. One or two younger guys are with him. The men begin to talk about the rain and how grateful they are for it has come after a long wait.

I wait. They drink and talk about everything but what matters. I wait. Watching them, I realize that the knife is no longer so heavy in my pocket. It is in fact thirsting, like myself, for the blood of another. And I shall oblige. I wait. I think of my earlier thoughts of how redundant the cycle of blood is. But it does not matter to me now. The neon blue moonlit memory of Jeremiah's death spins rapidly to the front of my mind as I watch the large man excuse himself from the seated ring. He says he has to go "milk the donkey" and all the men laugh. My heart kicks as I wrap the devil's apron around my mind to protect it from the blood splatter that I anticipated. I am hugging the container of brew as the man approaches me. He steps over my out stretched legs, off the veranda and round to the back of the building. Realizing that I don't have much time, I place the alcohol beside me and follow behind him. In the darkness I make out the man's form. He is standing next to one of the blair toilets unzipping. I hear his trickle splashing onto the ground to compliment the rain. He sighs and speaks to me.

"Here to milk the donkey as well?" he laughs at his joke.

I stagger towards him while pulling the knife discretely from my pocket.

"Not too close now, *shasha*, you don't want to..." his sentence is cut off by the rusty blade digging into his Adam's apple.

His hoarse gurgle lets me know in the darkness that my first attack was good. I slam his face against the wall of the toilet and he falls to his knees with his hand clutching his throat. I grab his hair, stand over him and stab his neck again and again as his left hand pushes against my face, helpless. I feel the warmth of his blood from his hand on my face and the spurts from his neck. Slowly, he slides grotesquely to the muddy ground, his breath leaving him. I fling the knife into the darkness. Leaving him twisting in pangs of death in the mud, his penis hanging out of his trousers, his blood washing away in the rain with eroding soil, I wash my hands and face quickly at a faucet on the back wall of the bar. I walk behind the bar, avoid the veranda and walk up the gravel road to the bus stop where I caught the bus when I was a child leaving the village. This time will leave and there will be no little Jeremiah chasing me. Just the tinkling slivers of rain and the black jade of night. I remember Jeremiah's request after my first night back, forget me, he had said. As I wait outside for the bus to leave, the rain is washing away the blood from the trench coat. I like the rain right now; it is soft on my face.

* * *

Symphony Scorpions

"The big man was dead, the Weaver continued to walk the path alone. It is hard to walk a path alone. Your greatest enemy becomes yourself, but also your greatest friend." *Ambuya's* voice is more like a brooding,

"He follows a vision of the Oracle to a large lake – a lake as still as and quiet as it is beyond the grave. The moon is setting at the end of the lake and light is lifting its head from the other end of the earth. The vision of the oracle walks into the water. The Weaver waits."

Around us the night is rubbing itself against the walls of the hut from the outside. And from the inside the fire is flickering to hold up the walls. Tonight I am unwell; I had been stung by a little black scorpion while playing on the rocks at the back of the compound. I had spent much of the day lying in the kitchen wrapped in *Ambuya's* itchy-scratchy blanket consumed in a swirl of fever and delirium. Now I am barely conscious, trying not to miss the end of the story. I lift my head out of the lake of dreams and freakish hallucinations occasionally so I can breathe the clean air of reality before I sink back into confusion. My grandfather is here, seated in his usual place on the bench. He is grinding more leaves in a little wooden bowl. With this he will make more of the potion I have been drinking all day to fight the poison of the scorpion. He grunts at *Ambuya*, who goes on her knees, leaves my side and takes the bowl out of *Sekuru's* shaky hands. She scrapes the pulp into the little pot on the fire.

"The other one is ready," his words reach me as an echo far away.

"Yes," her voice sounds like the whisper of a river.

His coarse hands shakily unwrap me. He makes me sit up as he takes his place behind me leaning against the wall. I sit between his thighs facing the fire. I feel the chill of being unwrapped. I hear the metallic clang of a rusty, profusely steaming pot placed before me. And before I know it darkness envelops me in the form of the blanket. The pot is under it with me, so is grandfather, behind me, holding me. As the steam fills the blanket I feel the fear of suffocation. But *Sekuru's* hands are strong. He has a hold of both my arms. I let out a moan.

"Breathe," he says strongly, "breathe."

Tears roll down my cheeks along with sweat as my body becomes weak. I give up my struggling and let the sour steam rush into my lungs. I feel them burn and relax; my insides become soggy as they too begin to burn. My grandfather's voice is still echoing in my mind, telling me to breathe. As the burning rises within, I begin to feel things crawling on my skin. Scorpions! I begin to fight but his arms are strong. I call out for my grandmother, hoping that my voice reaches beyond the blanket. But she does not hear me. The talons of panic claw at me in the darkness. I am going to die! Hundreds of red scorpions are crawling all over my skin and my grandfather becomes a monster with large heavy arms telling me to breathe. My voice becomes hoarse from yelling and I am tried of struggling. Slowly the scorpions leave my skin. The blanket is lifted and the flickering of the fire finds its way to my eyes. I collapse sideways heaving. *Ambuya* rushes forward.

"Don't be afraid, my child, they are all gone," her voice is a stern whisper.

"Scorpions," I mutter.

Sekuru has risen arduously, and is seating himself back in his spot, he is wiping sweat from his brow with his cloth. Ambuya wraps me in the blanket again and begins to make me drink the warm liquid of ground herbs.

"See now, my child, this will make you better," I wince at the bitterness, "no more scorpions, see?"

Grandfather- spent - is snorting snuff into each nostril. He is no longer a monster with heavy arms. He is old and tired. When I finish drinking, I lie down.

"So, the Weaver waited at the edge of the lake," She continues as though nothing had occurred, "but just before the sun rose, he saw her. The Daughter - his daughter. She walked out of the lake just as the Oracle had walked in. Little ripples made way for her as she walked out. Water coursed down her body, which was heavily adorned in talismans and beads. Her hair was of clay coated locks. Anyone else would not have recognized her, but what father would not recognize his daughter? But her eyes looked like she was blind. She walked right past her father in silence and headed for the path back into the forest. It was then that the Basket Weaver wept. All the tears that had lain undisturbed in the drying pasture of is heart, they came forth. They had matured over the years like beer to be offered to the ancestors. And now he let them loose crying for the death of his daughter. The old man fell to his knees in agony, his grief churning his insides. It was then that his daughter turned and looked at him. He saw her, her eyes still blind but watching him. He stopped his weeping. He knew that she had seen him. And she was his daughter. So he followed her quietly knowing that they would walk till she came to a village that only she knew. And there she would become the Oracle. So they walked. The Basket Weaver followed his daughter – the Oracle."

She sighs and adjusts the blanket that is wrapping me,

"You see, my child, there are no more scorpions. Now rest, and let your dreams be kind to you, rest." She pats me softly on the shoulder

* * *

A giant raindrop falls in slow motion silence and lands in a deafening groaning explosion clearing the dust on the ground and spraying a fertile scent of soil in all directions. Papermoon fancies are freed in my memories of dark-skinned sadness. The blue night paints my vision with languid longing and compressed laughter. I have become a ghost sitting at the edge of the forest waiting for things that will not come. I am seated in Julia's kitchen on this strange night where a light rain still allows for the moonlight to shine through. The moon reflects my thin string of regrets that hang like beads of dew on a spider's web. A glass of scotch in my left hand – neat and full.

"I can feel it in my bones," she says, "I am going to die young." Julia is standing above the kitchen sink rubbing a little water on the back of her neck.

I like the way she smells right now – soft in a most peculiar way. Her daughter is asleep. The window reveals the progress of the battle between cloud cover and moonlight. The clouds may be triumphing. She strides up and down the kitchen in a nippy pace that makes her seem to be spread all over the room.

"Do they know it was you?"

"You may want to sit down,"

She comes and sits across from me at the table.

"What will you do?"

"Leave,"

"How?"

"It's in the works,"

"You don't strike me as the violent type,"

"I don't,"

"The newspaper makes it seem like they don't know,"

"They will take their toll at the varsity,"

"They mention you in the paper as an instigator, well not you personally, but your work."

"Do they?"

"Why didn't you tell me you were a writer?"

"You never asked,"

She laughs quietly. I down the glass of whiskey in two flaming gulps and rise to get another. As I am pouring myself a glass by the counter, she comes up behind me and puts her arms around my stomach. Her hands are holding me a little tightly and her face is buried in the groove of my back. I feel her breathe in deeply. The bottle of whiskey is almost empty when I put it back on the counter. I turn around and kiss her. She sighs.

"You taste like whiskey,"

"You taste like water." I say.

"When do they arrive?"

"Soon."

"I guess this is it, then."

"I guess so."

After a few minutes, my publisher arrives. His eyes are excited and he has a broad grin that exposes his uncared for brown tobacco teeth. In fact, he carries the scent of expensive tobacco on his checkered shirt. His blue jeans and suede shoes are no exception. His mood is a little too happy considering the events.

"You look a tad too spiffy, ole' chap," I comment

"Are you kidding me?" he snorts, "This is history in the making, I haven't had this much excitement in my life since the liberation struggle. I used to help heroes – at least they were back then - to and fro across the border."

"I see,"

"By golly, mate, you have no idea what an itch you've been to these buggers, hey." He scratches his wispy grey hair.

"Would you like a drink?" Julia offers.

"Well," snort, "we're a bit tight on time," he licks his lips, "But if you insist."

She pours him the rest of the whiskey,

"Rocks?"

"Ha!" he virtually grabs the glass out of her hands, and tosses it down in a single motion, "Fuckin' good that is," he turns to me, "Shall we?"

"Yeah,"

He turns and walks out the door. I turn to Julia who is leaning against the counter and looking at the floor. I give her a timid hug. I like the way she smells, soft in a peculiar sort of way. While we kiss, her hand grips my collar violently, desperately. But when we pull our faces apart, she is smiling.

"You want to hear my secret?" she whispers.

"You can tell me when I come back," I kiss her again and leave.

Outside, in the dark, I locate my publisher by the glow of his cigarette. He is by his car puffing like a Soweto coal train. He hops into the car energetically making it bounce a little.

"Plane leaves in three hours, assuming nothing goes wrong, you'll be on it." He snickers, "I got a bag of clothes for you, hope they fit, and I got your documents in there too. Good thing you keep your passport with me huh?"

Bloody publishers. Always hyped about action. I think it's because they bear some form of immunity. Nobody is going to kill a publisher; no, they'll just pop the fucking writer. I have always put publishers in the same boat as Western journalists, you know -the fuckers that feed parasitically on the suffering of others, just taking pictures and winning prizes. Why the fuck do so many war journalists make it out of war alive? The few that do get killed are probably the ones who have come to take the job more seriously and hope to make a difference, then they get popped and that is probably because they started to care. Now here I am with my half-British-half-Australian publisher who is saving my hide. I am still amused by how his accent floats in the grey area that is kind of Briton-slash-Aussie-slash-Boer. He tosses his cigarette butt out the window as we drive. The roads are empty. He immediately lights another one. Both his hands are on the wheel. And the fag is on auto-pilot between his lips. His eyes are on the roads and he is sitting completely upright. He is a tallish man, freckled beyond recognition by the African sun and glad to be. He often complains about the English weather even though he goes there frequently to visit family. He always tells me how his family asked him to leave Zimbabwe and come live with them and he laughed and told them they could keep their potatoes and soggy weather.

"You, really are something, you know that," he says without looking at me, "I think that people like you are the future of this country. And don't get me wrong, mate, I'm not trying to patronize neither. You're too bright for that."

I have also always liked how he can use the Aussie "mate" next to the British "bloke" only to follow it with the Boer "man" all in the same paragraph and have no qualms about it.

"Anyway, man," he says, "When you get out there, don't let those blokes fuck with you coz they will. Fucking ignorant blighters they are. They'll see your skin and that's all they'll see. They'll ask you if you speak African, and why your English is so good, and if you have running water in your house." He laughs to himself, "But don't let them get to you. Just show them like it is…"

He takes in a deep inhalation then chucks the defeated smoke out the window. I can tell his mind is far off. He is reaching into his jacket for another fag. I don't think I have ever seen him this edgy.

"There'll be some one waiting for you when you get off the plane. And don't worry you'll be ok, just learn to play the game and you'll be fine. That's all it is out there, man. A game. In here it's different, it's life or death, but out there, it's just a game." He is desperately trying to teach me everything I need to know about being out of the country in twenty minutes forgetting that I have ventured out before, "Give me a call if you need anything yeah? I'll be there to check up on you in a week or two. This is assuming it all works out at the airport. They could be waiting for you, but I talked to some people and they thought we had a little leeway. So it should be okay. Oh, by the way the guise is that you've been called for the McCormick Lecture Series. Okay? McCormick…M-C,"

"Relax, you're making me edgy."

He laughs and I join him. What else can we do? So we laugh, then fall silent for the rest of the way. The street lights go by outside. They paint my departure orange; that is how I will remember it. If someone asks me how was your departure? I will say it was orange. That is how I left my country, on a dark orange night, with litter on the road sides. A quiet night, past people simmering in high–density hovels. It is empty except for the smog of fears that hover lazily over our hopes. A cool wind is entering and leaving the car through the open windows. I want to breathe this air one last time. Diesel fumes and dust along with scented memories of things I was not there to experience. I put my tongue out to see if I can taste anything. Even when it is on my tongue the dust will not surrender the secrets it carries. I put my palm out the window to touch the air and let it grace my skin once more.

* * *

Batons and sticks are landing heavily on dark, brown skin. Purple bruises and blood-splatter color the once white shirts as people fall to the dust. Everything is occurring under the patronage of tear gas. Knives, bricks, batons and sticks carry out the conversation that lips ought to have. I have been whisked away, much to my surprise by the bandana boys who were holding up the front line that was nose to nose with the riot officers. I suppose they had underestimated the civilian. In the instant after my crime the assembly became a tsunami that washed over the law enforcers and their dogs while they were still gulping in disbelief. But it did not take them too long to recover. In the treacherous fog of tear gas I briefly recognize the guy who had given me the wet rag, he is busily tying his own rag to his face. I do the same.

"Run!" I am told as I am being dragged by the five or six boys I had been in the company of earlier.

There is a barrage of song and frenzied destruction chasing us in the form of the supporters. Dogs bark and bones grind against fiberglass shields, women scream and the symphony of revolution completes itself wretchedly. We run across the park lawn which has become a field in which oppression is being cultivated in the fertile soil of corruption watered by futility. Flanking us and trying to cut us off is a group of municipal police and dogs. They probably want to close off our escape from the park to contain what will evidently be a disastrous occasion. But they will not catch us. We are jumping over the park fence and running blindly into the road. Cars swerve and screech to bouncing stops. A mild pile-up occurs involving three cars as we cross the four lanes and head straight for the urban center. About twenty of us have made it across the road before we see police vehicles, cutting off the escape of the rest of the people. Agents of the law are flying out of the vehicles before they come to a halt. The beatings ensue instantly as the stragglers are herded back into the park.

I catch a glimpse of a man pulled one way by an officer and in the other direction by a dog while two other officers are tenderizing him with kicks and punches. And as quickly as it begun, he is tossed into the back of a Santana and they sprint off after more vainly fleeing protesters. A few more officers are coming after us. My rescuers pull me once more by the collar. The experience is a flurry of movement through alleys and streets, buildings and yards. I have no idea where we are at all. I just follow speedily while begging my aching body to get its priorities straight. We pass through office buildings and offices taking the back stairwells. People look at us startled. I notice that some are dropping off as we run and taking their own directions. It's probably the smart thing to do. Then I realize we have reached First Street. There are three of us left. We are sweating, and we turn to look at each other as we are taking off our bandanas and rags from our heads and faces. The two boys smile at me then laugh. Looking around I realize that no one is giving us a single glance as they are walking about their business.

"It's been good guys," says one of the guys, slapping my back he turns and goes in his own direction hastily.

"Till the next time, hey? Ha ha." The other chap wipes the sweat off his face as he is turning to leave.

"Thanks," I say.

"For what?" he says slyly and winks.

Now seems a good time to make myself scarce and find an alibi. I stop and buy myself a bottle of brandy before I walk – as casually as possible – to my publisher's office. About me, a harmonious combination of elements moulds itself before my eyes and becomes a symphonic view of hurtful guarantee. A naughty wind is still sprinting about the city. Sweat-tickled faces are floating above the ground on quiet soles. Mine is one of them but on soles a little less than quiet.

* * *

Sequin and Solipsism

We pass under the Independence monument. That is how we know we are almost at the airport. The huge geometric structure arched solidly over the road ending in a raised split scorpion tail or is it a forked tongue? It has a very seventies, modernistic architecture look to its fickle fortitude. On it, above our heads: Independence 1980 – in the big bold confidence that must have, at one time, mirrored the feeling of the masses. The celebrations were intense. The hope and implications were infinite. Bob Marley even came and did a concert. We were new and fresh, hip and happy. We threw off the leash of Rhodesia and beaded our identity with the adornment of Zimbabwe. We reconciled with our oppressors immediately, because we are a forgiving people and we held hands and began our expedition into the future. But that period seems to have lasted as long as it takes us to pass under this monument. I have been told that someone tried to burn the monument down shortly after its completion. That is why they had to put up a little guard shed by it for a while. To fend off those political dissidents.

But my memory of these times, the time of our own little mini-holocaust –are but a blur for I was only twitching and convulsing in my post embryonic stages. Apparently I was "born free". Freely born into neocolonialism and the even more wretched intra-colonialism. It is only logical that when one has run out of external enemies they must conjure up, or better yet make-belief of the enemies lurking within their own siblings. So we have we have come from there to this. As we pull into the airport parking lot, to join the thirty-odd cars that are already there, the air becomes less friendly. I lick my lips and get out of the car. My publisher finishes off a cigarette as he pulls my bag out and locks the doors. The airport is deathly silent, it is the international airport, but the rest of the world will not fly here for whatever reason. Only two or three airlines, including the country's, use the place which is a shame because it is a great building with lots of wonderful stone sculptures in it as examples of our fine contemporary artists.

"Well, here goes nothing." He says heaving a sigh and heading for the entrance.

"Fucking shit," I sigh and yawn.

I always yawn when I'm nervous. Our footsteps echo against the shiny granite exterior of the building as we approach. I look left and right before crossing from the car park to the side of the building. There are no cars, this is more an attempt to delay the eventuality. My publisher is pulling out his cell phone with his free hand and dialing shakily. He puts the phone to his ears and coughs while listening.

"Yup, we're there mate," he says suddenly, "yeah… I know. Well, I'll let you know…we'll see. Alrighty then." And he hangs up.

"Last wishes?"

"I should be asking you that, man!" he laughs, "just making a phone call to make sure we're on track…and to let people know where we are."

"Hmm." I get the idea.

This is me. I write. This is where dark twisted roads have brought me – to kneel before the monument of language. And because I write with black ink on white paper, my thoughts are of black ink on white paper. If I wrote on brown skin with golden tears, then my thoughts would be of golden tears on brown skin. They would flow out of the eyes of promise and down the cheeks of night's face and leave a little recalcitrant trail of things we'll soon forget. Then they'd sail downwards through silent air and land with a mineral tinkle of doubt. This is me. I write. I do not stand in the street throwing bricks that crumble like dried bodies of betrayed children against the Great House of Stone. Nor do I cheer and shout and sing loud- ly before the cameras of journalists who will print my picture in the National Geographic for lazy minds to caress. I sit at a desk, hunch over and squeeze drops of fire from my eyes for my fingers to translate. That is what I do – that is me. I am not a hero who traverses the adverse jungle on my belly towards freedom. I sit at my desk and weave stories for people to use. They can use my stories to carry water or food in, or as a mat to sit or sleep on while they dream. I weave reeds of experience from many rivers and swamps into something useful to forget. I give people something to forget about.

The florescent blue light of the airport interior has a con- cupiscent self-containment. I walk up to the checking counter with my one, leather bag, big enough for hand luggage. The lady at the counter is pleasant, but tired. Her blue uniform is complemented well by her flamboyant scarf even though she has a little too much make-up on. The braided extensions on her head glitter dubiously as she busies herself at the computer screen typing rapidly. I decide to check my bag in. She smiles and hands me my boarding pass.

We wait for what seems an eternity after checking in. I am tapping my ticket nervously against my knee. There is about half an hour before I have to leave the company of my publisher to go into the boarding area. That is the part I am more concerned about. I will be alone when I go through and there will be another half hour to wait before actually boarding the flight then another twenty minutes before take off. All this waiting just gives more room – more time – for calamity. And in the meantime I will torture myself by stewing in my apprehensions of encumbrance. My publisher sits next to me with his arms folded, his blue eyes scanning the environment.

"Let's go out for a smoke," he says, "in fact let's go up to the waiting lounge and smoke there."

And so we rise, and head for the stairs, in the pale blue-white of the light. Our footsteps echo in the great hall as we pass kiosk after kiosk, all closed of course. There are about sixty other people in the whole space, and each conversation echoes coldly – clinically - to reinforce the emptiness of the building. There are probably more people working here than actually taking flights. We go up the stairs to the smoking lounge where we can see the tarmac and the planes waiting to leave. There are two planes, preparing for boarding and one is taking off as we arrive. The high-pitched engine blast digs into my ears and I wince. We walk out to the balcony and light cigarettes as the plane is turning onto its runway. It is very loud. The air is cool and giving its consent to the sound, the concrete smells thick and rough. My publisher is smoking and leaning on the bar of the balcony and I look at him. He is relieved to be inhaling the tobacco again. I think to myself that this man has probably smoked, in a single night, enough to contaminate his entire posterity quite sufficiently. His hair gambols lightly in the breeze. The metal bar is cold when I lean on it. Watching him, I tenderly experience the blink of an eye as I breathe through his life. He won't leave, even though he could, I think quietly. Yet there are those that are dying to leave even though they have never seen anything outside of this country. Maybe some deranged solipsism keeps him here preferring to rule in hell than to serve in heaven. He helped liberation heroes run back and forth and has stood in the line of fire for things that some believe have nothing to do with him. I watch him watch the plane leap sonorously into the sky - his blue eyes a little watery.

"Why don't you leave?" I speak with a heavy rock in my voice.

"Why don't you stay?" he does not look at me.

"You shouldn't leave."

"You shouldn't stay."

I suppose this what Zen enlightenment feels like: A tumble of rocks down a hill followed by a great silence and settling dust in which you find a single glorious sequin of no value but contentment. The rest of the wait is in silence. When the time comes he walks me to the entrance of the boarding area. We go back down the stairs and I have my pass, my passport, and a wad of American dollars he gave me. He had said it was an advance for the things I will do. I give him a gruff handshake as men do and he slaps my shoulder solidly to compensate for the sensitivity we cannot show. His blue-green eyes are watery.

"I will wait till the flight leaves just incase." He says, "Someone will tell me if you make it."

"See you soon ole chap," I force a smile.

Turning in to the entrance, I hear footsteps rushing towards us. I turn and see three men in grey suits striding briskly towards us. A painful spike ignites in my chest and I bleed from the inside. The first man is of average height and a little thin.

His cheekbones stick out distinctly. The other two are a little stockier; the first, tall with a thick mustache and the other bald and stout, but this does not take away from the imposition of his demeanor. They stop before us silent for a moment.

"Sir," says the thin one who is clearly the leader, "you'll have to come with us."

"What's this about?" says my publisher sounding outraged in the way white people always do when they are confused.

"Let's not make a scene, sir." He says with danger pulsing in his voice.

I privately think that I will definitely create a scene. The refractory ardor is already in motion within me. Having already been labeled a profligate in their cant, I assume they would expect no less from me. His two goons flank him and I position my legs to support my center of gravity. Fucking feds. My body becomes cold and I feel a tickle in my ears. My heartbeat rises to my throat. My publisher stands in front of me with his aging chest protruding to give of a false confidence.

"We have our rights," he says as if people's rights matter on this turf. "We want our lawyer to be..."

The two large men advance towards him. Funny how white folk, no matter how long they have been in the country, think a lawyer will solve all their problems. I pull him aside as I ready myself to erupt. Some things cannot be quantified, like the extent of my dislike for these men, or what they stand for. I remember in boarding school, one boy ran so fast that we quantified his speed to be equal to that of six dogs and a pregnant bitch following behind with difficulty. I can already see it - lucidly: me in a small, white room with a rusty table over which a naked light bulb is sizzling, the skinny man in the grey suit with bad breath and his fucking tie askew, questioning me in some arcane colloquy that is more ritual than necessity.

Followed by the shit I went through before. A bag over my face smelling like many faces. And I disappear again in the back of a vehicle past yellow streetlights in the company of malignant shadows to the land of cold walls and damp floors. To the odor of human innards and blood – to pain. No, I'm not going back there. The flashbacks vanish as quickly as they came.

All three men are a little red eyed to forewarn us of their malign proclivity. But I'm not going back there. I am tired of being afraid. I drop my ticket and passport on the floor and they land with a slap that echoes mournfully into the vortex of the inevitable. I recall that the knees are the weakest part of a large man. They approach with their hands reaching for me like thick roots of devastation. Their grey suits reflect a silken blue light. And my publisher is pulling up next to me in slow motion. Then suddenly a sharp whistle slides crisply through the air followed by,

"Hey Champion!" I drop my jaw in surprise at the intruder, "Excuse me a moment gentlemen."

It is John walking in all confidence as always, black leather jacket, grey trousers, shiny shoes, and the golden wristwatch glittering with promise. His belly is pushing out of his jacket to reveal a black shirt. The large men stop as though to acknowledge rank. They hesitate. John does not look at me as he goes directly the skinny agent and hands him the cell phone he is carrying as priest would a chalice.

"News from the top, *shasha.*" He slaps the phone in the confused man's palm.

The man composes himself and puts the phone to his ear. The two others take the opportunity to lunge and grab me from either side. I do not struggle - yet. John still doesn't look at me. In fact he pulls out his handkerchief and wipes the imaginary sweat from his brow. He raises his wrist and looks at his watch as though this is taking too long – as though he is annoyed by the gravity of time.

"Yes…I understand, sir. Affirmative…yes sir." The skinny man is not fazed.

He returns the phone to John and looks to his two sidekicks.

"Release him," As he is speaking a mobile phone rings.

He pulls his own phone out of his jacket inside pocket.

"Yes sir, we have been alerted. No problem, sir."

His expression still has not changed, as though he is accustomed to the impermanence of his delegations. I can feel the eyes of a few watchers in the hall looking in our direction.

"There has been an error." Then painfully, "We apologize for the inconvenience."

He glances quickly at John who pretends not to notice. And with the same echoing stride, the three men head towards the exit with an expansive lack of remorse. The skinny man speaks to the other two quietly and quickly as they walk. I turn towards John who is watching the men leave. He pats his brow with the kerchief as he turns towards my befuddled publisher and me. He strides towards me and pats my back jovially.

"If you're not out of here within an hour, there's little more I can do, Champion, hey?"

"I see," I say blankly.

"Well, let's not get all emotional now," he mocks, "I just heard something in the pipeline and thought I'd look into it."

"Thanks, man."

"Like I said, Champion: no saints and martyrs, just practical people. Don't say thank you. Consider this an investment in the Future, no?" He laughs.

As I pat him on the back, I see that the three men have not left. The skinny one is standing by the entrance, the bald one pacing by the exit and the third standing conspicuously a few meters away watching us. Watching me. My publisher has picked up my passport and ticket off the floor, he hands them to me. As I turn John grabs my shoulder, and in a most confidential tone, he places something cool in my hand.

"And give this to Lee, I never got the chance." He does not look me in the eye.

I take the locket and pocket it.

"I'll see what I can do."

"Just when I had gotten you a farm too, huh." He sighs mockingly, "Well I guess I'll just have to consolidate it. You know where to find me, champion."

"Well, that was jolly exciting," my publisher finally regains composure, "Alrighty, mate, let's try that again shall we." He pats my back gesturing towards the gate, "The sooner the better, my friend." He gives me a gentle but urgent pat-shove towards the counter.

Turning around with a smile, I breathe in deeply, and walk through the gates and show my ticket to the sleepy man who eyes me suspiciously. My hand is still shivering from the adrenaline and my head feels light. I pass through the turnstile. I turn once more and see John and my publisher standing side by side though worlds apart. My publisher reaches into his jacket and pulls out a smoke and sticks it between his lips. John pats his forehead with his handkerchief and pockets it. I smile to myself and turn away. That's right, we don't say goodbye because we are all on the same path to different places – a contorted testament of kinship.

* * *

"The Weaver followed his daughter back through he forest. He knew that he was headed back to the Village. He thought that the Village would banish him because he had freed the large man and fled. But he walked on. The Daughter was to replace the old diviner that had walked into the water to the City of Oracles to rest. She would become the village oracle. Soon they were out of the forest and the sun glared down at them. The Weaver was pleased to be back in the familiar landscape near the Village. They walked on, the Daughter leading the way. They did not speak, the Weaver had learnt not to speak. The land was different. The grass was not as tall as he had remembered it. And the river could no longer be heard from the path outside the village. The wind was dry and no birds greeted them as they came. On entering the village, his daughter headed for the oracle cave and he for his compound, without a word.

"When he got there, he saw his home was crumbling, there were no chickens and goats running about in the yard, no children's laughter. And his weaving stool lay in decay against the side of his hut. His wives came out and greeted him as a stranger, but on approaching him they recognized him. They fell to the floor weeping with joy. They wept so loud that they drew the neighbors who also did not recognize him at first. But they had changed. He had changed. The Forest had changed his eyes. And he could see how their hearts had grown smaller and shriveled in the heat of the sun. That night his wives told him many things about who had died and who had been born. That there had been another plague of field mice and locusts. That there had been no oracle to turn to, so the Village had crumbled. The elders had become senile and desperate. They blamed many people. That they had killed the Weaver's neighbor for pointing out that the Reed Flute Traveler had not been repaid for ridding them of the first plague. They decried him as one who wished to replace the oracle. His wives also told him of how they had been ostracized after he had fled the Village. He remained silent and simply nodded his head and sighed gazing into the fire."

Ambuya gazed in to the obedient flame surrounded by embers. Jeremiah and I sat helplessly as the gyre of change washed over us. *Ambuya* was sad as she always was at the end of a tale. *Ambuya* let the night creep into the hut tonight to share the end of the tale. She did not put more wood in the fire, and we did not try to. We watched her intently with sinking hearts. Sitting with Jeremiah I knew this would probably be the last story we'll be told. We were too old for stories now. In the great silence, Night came and held grandmother's face in both palms. It rubbed itself against my elbow and threw an arm over Jeremiah's shoulder.

"He just sighed and gazed at the fire. His wives asked where he had gone. And he said that he was looking for their child. Did you find her? They asked, Did you return with our daughter? He gazed at the fire. His wives pressed on timidly. I returned with an oracle, he responded finally. And his wives burst into tears knowing that now they could cry. They wept and held each other in the gaze of the dying fire. That night the Weaver did not slept. He sat in silence till night began to walk away. And in that dawn, the elders and other villagers stormed the compound angrily."

Her voice shivers; the room becomes darker as Night presses against the single flame that remains faithful to the story. The flame slowly lets go and night fills the room allowing only the glow of embers. *Ambuya* becomes an orange spirit seated in the fluid shroud of night that dances about her like the fire once did.

"They banished him for rescuing the *Zindoga*. They sent him away from the village with sticks and stones. They also blamed him for the plague and the ruin of the Village. They spat on him and beat him with sticks. Some of the villagers bowed their heads in shame. His wives wept and tore at their clothes and his children wept. Nobody spoke to the oracle. But what more can a father do than bring his daughter back home? They sent him away. He left and went back to the forest path. That night he met again with the large baboon on the path. The great monster of his fears. Now tell my grandchildren: What becomes of a man who faces Fear alone on the forest path? Where would he go?"

I know the tale is done. Jeremiah is spell bound and the embers are contemplative. They are succumbing both to the darkness of the conclusion and that of night.

"Rest well, children," *Ambuya* whispers.

With that she rises, silently with graceful difficulty. The blanket wrapped around her becomes her cloak of mystery complementing the tenebrosity. She moves out of the hut like a memory. At the door of the hut she becomes a part of the night and disappears. This is how I will remember her for the rest of my life, as a secret that moves in the wind and comes alive with night. She once said that in the instant before a person dies, their soul steps away from the body to witness its own liberation. And I wonder what happens if you are all soul like grandmother, what happens then? Jeremiah and I are left seated in the darkness of glowing embers memories and dreams coming alive, flowing from us and forming a puddle that consumes us both.

* * *

Dreaming of where kisses and quiet don't matter so you too
Can be lonely and not be bothered
Where riot police can drive by chanting death and smashing boots
To jaws and still you can be smiling and wondering
What a flower is
Distracted but only briefly

-For those who have encouraged me
continually to discover who I am.

Made in the USA
Lexington, KY
21 February 2011